Carolyn,

Don't Push
Sunrise Series

(5)

BOBBY BRIGHT
MEETS HIS MAKER:
THE SHOCKING TRUTH
IS REVEALED

BY
John R. Brooks

[signature]

2017

ILLUSTRATIONS BY
**Dan Daly, Troy Gustafson
and Jeff Elliott**

Old Farm Press

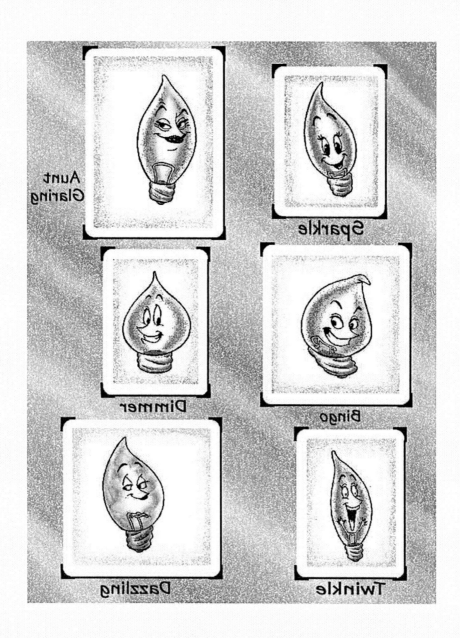

Contents

Our Family Picture

Prologue

It was nearly seven o'clock in the morning. Mr. McGillicuddy rolled over on his side and saw the time on the digital clock: 6:58 a.m., July twenty-eighth.

He couldn't believe it. It was nearly four o'clock when he and Mrs. McGillicuddy had finally gotten into bed, and here he was lying awake and wide-eyed and staring at the clock. "I should be dead tired and sound asleep. This is definitely jet lag," he whispered to himself.

It was the same feeling he had when he and Mrs. McGillicuddy had returned from their Christmas visit to Spain last January.

"No need to wake up, Jane," he muttered to himself, as he looked across the bed to the other side, where his wife lay motionless, snoring softly and obviously very much asleep.

I wonder if she is okay, he thought and reached over and patted her arm gently. She stirred ever-slightly and shifted her body for a brief moment.

"Well, I guess I will get up," he said to himself and crawled out from underneath the light sheet. He had pulled it over him about twenty minutes ago when he had awoken to a chill in the room. When they had arrived from the airport at two thirty and unlocked the garage door, the blistering heat felt like it was coming from an oven. He had immediately switched on the air conditioning system and set the thermostat as low as possible. It had taken nearly four hours for the house to cool off after sitting empty for the past month.

After brushing his teeth and washing his face, he walked to the kitchen and put the brown grounds into the coffeemaker. He grimaced when he entered the hallway between the dining room and the kitchen. Four pieces of luggage and three large sacks were scattered across the floor. Inside two of those suitcases were lots of dirty clothes that needed to be washed or sent to the cleaners. The sacks and one suitcase were filled with many new sweaters, beautiful *Lladro* porcelain figurines, and other souvenirs from the McGillicuddy's second trip to Spain in less than a year. It would take forever, he was certain, to find a place in the house for everything.

Looking at all that work ahead was enough to make him shiver for a moment. Jane had already told him on the flight home that just because, for the first time ever, they had failed to do spring-cleaning in April did not mean that it wasn't going to happen. She intended to clean the house from top to bottom once they had rested up from the trip.

He knew she meant business too, because she mentioned it more than once during the return flight from

Madrid. He was certain it was going to happen and he wasn't happy about it. If there was ever anything John McGillicuddy truly detested doing, it was spring-cleaning.

He grabbed a cup from the cupboard and poured himself the black liquid he hoped would give him courage. After taking a couple of sips, he realized the coffee was too hot. He had burned the tip of his tongue, but the pain had given him an idea.

Maybe if he got a lot of work done and a lot of things taken care of while she slept, maybe he could change her mind. First, he would empty the suitcases and take the necessary clothes to the cleaners. The other stuff that needed to be laundered, he would stuff in the clothes washer.

Then, he thought he would try to sneak quietly around the house and place some of the souvenirs on bookshelves or anywhere else they might look good. By now, he had managed to drink two cups of coffee, and he liked his plan. He hoped it would prevent spring-cleaning.

He quickly stood up and walked to the hallway. He carried Mrs. McGillicuddy's new suitcase into the foyer and opened it. There were only clean clothes in this one, and it was the suitcase where he had packed Remington's Christmas tree lights. He would start with them. They were going back in the ornament box in the closet with all the other strands of lights.

He unzipped the flap and saw the bulbs. He could see the rubber band wrapped two or three times around them. "You're going back into the closet, little fellows, and don't try to escape this time." He pulled the strand from the suitcase.

As he did it, he felt a chill run down the center of his spine. Snuggled against the edge of the rubber band in the middle of the folded strand was the blue bulb. It appeared to be staring at him. "I know that's you, Bobby. I'm still grateful for what you did for me at that castle." Then he stepped away from the suitcase and shook his head. "Listen to me! I'm actually thanking a Christmas tree light bulb, and what is worse, I need to."

He smiled and headed for the foyer. Just as he arrived at the closet door, an idea popped into his head. He stopped and looked at the bulbs in his hand. "Maybe you don't want to go back in the closet, eh?"

Instead of opening the door, he turned and walked across the foyer and stopped on the staircase landing. He removed the rubber band and began unwinding the cord as he started climbing up the stairs.

"This will be perfect," he mumbled. "You little bulbs got to stay on the windowsill in Remington's room in his Madrid apartment, so why not the same treatment here? I can just walk across the room and put you on Remington's little tree when we decorate it the day after Thanksgiving."

He pulled the curtain away from in front of the corner window. "See, nobody will see you here. We hardly ever open these curtains or look out this window except when Remington visits."

"John, what in the world are you doing up there? Are you talking to yourself?"

Mr. McGillicuddy jumped when he heard her voice at the bottom of the stairs. He quickly crisscrossed the strand into three layers and placed it along the windowsill.

"Did you hear me, John?"

"Yes, dear. I was just checking to see if everything was okay up here."

He heard her clomping up the stairs, and he quickly moved the curtain back in place so the bulbs couldn't be seen. He walked out of the room and nearly bumped into her.

"Do you have to talk to yourself when you check to see if the house is okay?"

"Oh, stop it," he said. "I see you couldn't sleep either."

"No, I couldn't. But, I am still tired."

"It's part of jet lag, Jane."

1

Spring-cleaning in the Summer

In over thirty years of marriage, Mr. McGillicuddy remembered it only happened twice.

"Why does it have to happen a third time, Jane?" He had whined and griped all day yesterday, but to no avail. Two days after getting home from a marvelous three weeks in Spain, they were going to do *major* house cleaning. That meant doing even more than they did every year in a normal spring-cleaning session. It meant indoors and outdoors and even cleaning a building that wasn't part of the house. He had tried to talk her out of it, but finally he realized he could only grumble for so long before Mrs. McGillicuddy would put her foot down and say, "That's enough!"

"Well, that was yesterday. Maybe I can get lucky today and change her mind," he said to himself as he walked quietly upstairs to his office. It was just before eight o'clock and Mrs. McGillicuddy was still asleep. He took slow, cautious steps in hopes the stairs would not creak. He didn't want her to wake up any sooner than necessary.

Her words had been quite clear. "We are going to do all those other things we keep putting off each year. We have an upstairs closet that looks like a storage warehouse. When you open the door, something always falls out and hits you. The time has come for that to end. Plus, we are going to finally clean out that green shed next to the house. I can't imagine we are ever going to use the junk that has accumulated there."

"But why couldn't we wait until next spring and do it all then?" Mr. McGillicuddy mumbled to himself as he wandered into the upstairs guest room and looked at his enemy—the closet door.

He stood there staring at it for a moment and then started to leave and walk down the hall to his office. But, as he turned, he hesitated and a smile broke across his face.

"I know," he continued to visit with himself, "I will jump in here, clean out a few things, and maybe that will be enough for Jane to change her mind. Then, we could wait until next year."

He walked to the door and opened it. When he switched on the light, the bad news was right in front of him. He was staring at old suitcases, old framed pictures, some very old clothes, an ironing board, and some skis, plus lots and lots of boxes with papers hanging over the edges. There was no room to walk. There were empty hangers jammed together at one end of the clothes rod. There were half a dozen scrapbooks stacked in the corner to his left. There were hockey sticks that his son had used when he had played junior hockey over twenty years ago.

"Have you seen enough?"

He jumped three inches off the ground and swiftly turned around. "You scared the living tar out of me, Jane. How long have you been standing there?"

"Long enough to hear you mumbling, but also long enough to know that even you, the Mumbler, can't find words to describe how bad this closet looks."

At that moment, Mr. McGillicuddy accepted the truth. There was no chance that he could avoid what was about to happen.

"Yes, dear," he whined.

It was one o'clock. Mr. McGillicuddy was starving, and after enough moaning and groaning, he had convinced Mrs. McGillicuddy to go downstairs and fix them some lunch.

"I will do it on one condition," she had said. "You keep working here until I get the sandwiches fixed, and you understand that we are going to get all of this done today. That means when it cools down a little from that one-hundred-and-one-degree temperature outside, we are going to clean out that shed and get that junk to the curb before dark."

For a couple of seconds, Mr. McGillicuddy thought about saying he didn't like the conditions and would pass on eating lunch. However, he had quickly ended that thought when he kept hearing his stomach growl.

Now he heard her coming up the stairs. "What are you doing?" he said as he quickly stepped out of the room. He nearly bumped into her at the top of the landing.

"What do you mean, what am I doing? I'm bringing you your lunch."

"But, I thought I could come downstairs, and we could sit at the kitchen table and relax and enjoy the sandwiches."

Mrs. McGillicuddy laughed. "John, you never change. You want to get downstairs so you can turn lunch into at least a one-hour break. You can sit right there on that chair by the window, and I will sit on the piano stool. Here, take your plate. Enjoy."

He took the plate from her and stared at a big, thick sandwich with lettuce and bologna hanging out the sides of it. There was a hardboiled egg sitting next to it and about five large Ruffles potato chips.

"This is it? This is lunch?"

"Eat, John," she said and took a bite from her sandwich. "You know, dear, we have made a lot of progress. I can't believe we had kept all of those tax returns from over twenty years ago."

He started to answer, but she continued. "And, I think those skis can definitely find a home someplace else. And, I think..."

Mr. McGillicuddy nibbled on the egg and crunched on two chips. He stared into space and tried not to listen.

"So, do you agree?"

Mrs. McGillicuddy looked at her husband. He was staring through the window. "John, have you been listening to me? Do you agree?"

"Uh, sorry, dear. Sure, I agree," he said and put the third of the five potato chips into his mouth.

"Good. I'm done. That sandwich was good. Now you finish," she said and looked at his plate, which still had half of an uneaten sandwich and half of an uneaten egg. "I thought you were hungry."

"I've lost my appetite because of all the stuff that's still in the closet."

"Well, then eat up because you just agreed to go through those scrapbooks with me and see if there is anything we want to keep."

"What?" he said with a yelp. "I didn't agree to that."

"You just said, 'I agree.'"

"Well, I must not have heard you."

"You most certainly did hear me. You were looking right at me. So, last chance. Eat the rest of that sandwich right now so we can get started."

Suddenly, Mr. McGillicuddy was hungry. He took one bite and chewed it very slowly.

Mrs. McGillicuddy got up and walked back into the closet. She looked around at all the space. At least half of what had been in here was pure junk and was now lying at the curb outside, ready to be picked up by the trash service tomorrow. She lifted up three of the thick scrapbooks and started to walk out of the room.

"Bring those other three scrapbooks into your office," she ordered. "We can look at all of them in there."

"Well, let me finish my sandwich."

"John, nibbling on it won't make this go away. Finish the sandwich. We are going to look through all six of these together." She walked down the hall and put the scrapbooks on a desk in his office.

When she returned, Mr. McGillicuddy was still sitting there. "Now! Pick them up, John, and bring them. Let's go!"

He sighed and rolled his eyes upward toward the ceiling.

"And don't be so dramatic."

"I'm not being dramatic," he said. "I am just trying to digest my food and eat slowly."

She laughed and grabbed the plate from him and walked into the bathroom next door. "It will be sitting here by the sink if you get hungry again. But for now, you are helping me."

Over four hours later, after some laughter, a few occasional tears, a surprise or two, and even a few friendly arguments with his wife, Mr. McGillicuddy was ready to stop looking at pictures and clean out the shed—even if it was 100 degrees outside, even if it was *200 degrees* outside. It would still be better than looking at another scrapbook.

"Oh, my gosh! I had completely forgotten this. Look, John. Read this note."

"Do I have to? I've looked at pictures until my eyes are red. Now I have to read a letter."

"Quit acting like a spoiled child. You said you liked seeing all of these pictures again and reminiscing."

"No, I said that I liked some of the pictures and only the ones of you and me."

She laughed and gave him a slight nudge with her elbow. "You're just trying to make me feel good so I will tell you we are finished."

"That's a good idea. Let's stop. I've seen enough. We've been doing this for three hours already. Don't make me…"

Mrs. McGillicuddy interrupted him. "No, actually it's been a little more than four hours, dear."

"Even more reason. Please, please don't make me look through this final scrapbook, and I will give up. We'll keep all of this stuff. Put all of it back in the closet. I don't care. I will trip over them every time I walk in there. Even if I hurt myself, it will be worth it to not have to keep looking at pictures."

"You are unbelievable. Can you be any more dramatic?"

"Maybe." He laughed, and then with another dramatic sigh, he proclaimed, "Okay. The final moment of this thrilling adventure is here. A note I don't want to read, but I am going to read. Here, quickly give it to me. I can't wait any longer."

She shoved the wrinkled piece of stationery into his hand. "Read this, and we will quit."

"Promise?"

"Yes. Read it."

Mr. McGillicuddy smoothed out the wrinkles on the paper. "How did you read this all crumpled up?"

"Quit delaying, John. I read it between the wrinkles," she said. "So that means I will know if you are skipping over things. Read it!"

"Out loud? Are you serious?"

"Read it!"

He stared at the envelope. He saw it had been mailed from Calumet, Saskatchewan. "Wait a minute! Is this the letter from that distant cousin of mine? Gosh, how long ago was this?" He looked at the date on the envelope.

"Wow! Has it been fifteen years ago since that silly family reunion where I hardly knew any of the people there?"

When Mrs. McGillicuddy didn't answer, he looked up from the letter and said, "Was it that long ago?"

"Yes, it has been. I had forgotten, until I read the letter."

Mr. McGillicuddy looked at the piece of stationery and the envelope. Both were yellowing with age, and the paper was very brittle. He held it closer to his face and read.

> Dear John and Jane:
>
> It's very strange writing this letter to someone I barely know and yet can now think of as family.
>
> Since I don't really have anyone who I am close to and knew only a handful of people at the reunion, I was pretty well alone and wanted to return to Calumet when you folks sat down and talked. I have to admit, Jane, I was a little scared to say much because I hardly know anything about our "family."
>
> You were very pleasant, and I somehow figured out you were right. John and I are second cousins, although none of us really know much about the people who produced that relationship.

I am back at my factory and very busy and probably will never see you again, but it was nice to at least talk with someone in my so-called "family" who would listen and care.

Your cousin (I guess),
Robert McGillicuddy

"I remember him, vaguely. He sure seemed lonely."

"Yes, he did, John. In fact, that's the one thing I do remember about him. I haven't thought about this in a long time, but I know I felt very sorry for him. He was really lonely, and he said we were the only people who even bothered to visit with him."

"That whole trip was a waste of time," Mr. McGillicuddy grumbled. "Some families just aren't close. Ours never was, and I guess that's just another reason why I love you and Richard and Lisa and Remington so much."

"Yes, we have a very special, small family. I am fortunate to have a great brother and sister-in-law and two beautiful nieces. And I am so thankful for my two wonderful sisters. But remember, John, they are your family too, and they love you very much."

"Yes, I know. I've got just enough relatives on your side of the family, and I do like them." He folded the paper in half and put it inside the envelope and tossed it into the wastebasket.

"What are you doing?"

"I'm throwing it away," he answered. "We'll never see him again or talk to him. Why keep the note? It's like all our other scrapbooks. Half of the stuff is useless, but you never want to get rid of anything. We don't need this old letter."

"Explain to me," she said and placed her hands on her hips and stared at him, "what difference does it make? It's one tiny letter in a big book."

"Exactly my point, dear. We have too many of these 'big' books."

"Well, you listen to me, John McGillicuddy. Give that letter to me right now." She chuckled and added, "And I know you will, because if you do, I will agree to stop. We can call it a day."

Mr. McGillicuddy reached into the wastebasket and tossed the crumpled note back to her. "Here, take it. Take it before you change your mind."

"Thank you." She turned to walk away. "Put all those books back in the closet, and you are done for the day. I'm going to go fix you a nice, tasty dinner."

"All right," he shouted, "now we're cooking."

"No, I'm going to do the cooking." She smiled and, clutching the letter in her hands, started to leave the room.

But Mr. McGillicuddy just couldn't leave well enough alone. He tried one more time. "Aren't you going to put that letter back in here with all the other junk in this scrapbook?"

"No. I'm keeping it, and quit calling those scrapbooks 'junk.'" As she walked away, she looked back over her shoulder and said, "I have some other news for you."

She headed into the hallway, and just before she reached the landing at the top of the stairs, Mr. McGillicuddy stuck his head out the door and asked, "What other news? Please don't tell me you have changed your mind about us being finished?"

"No, I haven't changed my mind. We're through. You can relax."

"Then why do you have that mischievous look on your face?"

"I just thought of a great idea for Christmas. I will tell you when we have dinner."

2

No More Junk in the Garage

"**I**think yesterday and today are the two hardest days you have ever worked. You have been wonderful."

"I've loved every minute of it, dear. Knowing you, I'm sure you have more planned this afternoon." He managed to keep a straight face and not laugh. He was worn out from four hours of restarting, rearranging, and removing rakes, brooms, shovels, weed eaters, chain saws, hammers, wrenches, old used lawnmowers, and a hundred other things that were stored in the garage.

In many cases, he just moved some of the stuff from one place to the other. However, Mrs. McGillicuddy had definitely gotten her wish today. Much of the "junk," which she called almost everything in the garage, was now sitting next to the street. Once a month, there was a big trash pickup, and it was scheduled for tomorrow.

Of course, he grumbled the entire morning and tried to use aches and pains and hunger for excuses to stop working. However, he had only been successful once when they took a fifteen-minute break for lunch, and he got handed another bologna sandwich.

"Is that all we have to eat in this house?" he had moaned.

"The quicker you get finished today, the quicker you will eat a nice pot roast I have simmering on the stove."

Now that was enough to make a guy work as fast as possible. But even though he thought a lot about the tender meat that she always seasoned perfectly with special herbs and spices and how tasty the juicy carrots and potatoes would be, it didn't help speed up the cleaning process.

It was late afternoon. Mr. McGillicuddy groaned and said, "Eight hours of my life taken away." Then he groaned one more time and held his hands out in front of him with his palms upward. "Gone. I will never find those hours again, and all because of a few items out of place."

"We're finished, Mr. Drama King. You can go take a shower, and then we will have a wonderful dinner."

"Is the summer-cleaning-instead-of-spring-cleaning over?"

"Almost, dear. After dinner, we will finish upstairs."

It took a moment to register. He was stunned. He yelled, "What?"

"Don't shout like that," she scolded him. "Did you think we were going to just leave everything lying on the bed and the floor in the guestroom?"

"Oh, yeah," he quietly answered. "I guess we did leave that stuff outside the closet. I suppose we were still in shock about rediscovering a lost relative. And Jane, since I brought that back up, I think we need to talk some more about what you said last night. Are you sure you want to invite a man we have seen only once and not spoken to in the last fifteen years to spend Christmas with us?"

"We'll talk about it over dinner, but I'm not going to change my mind. Plus, John, he's your distant relative. I think it would be nice to call and ask him if he would join us for a few days at Christmas."

"We don't even know if he is alive."

"Then I guess a phone call would help us find out. Now, shoo! Go! Take your shower. Dinner is ready except for putting everything on the table. I'll putter around upstairs and put some things away until you finish. Then we will eat."

"Okay," he said. Suddenly, he felt better. He had two good reasons to take a longer shower than he normally did. One: he hoped Jane would get everything put away upstairs and back where it all belonged by the time he got out of the shower; and second: the hot water felt so good after lifting, pulling, hanging, and shifting stuff around in both the garage and that filthy shed all day.

He spent a great deal of the time singing loudly as the water rushed over his head, neck, and shoulders. He was a bit surprised that his wife had not already come downstairs and made him get out. Twice he started to turn off the water, but it felt so refreshing that he just stood there and enjoyed it flowing over him. Finally, he reluctantly finished and opened the shower door.

The moment he stepped onto the bathmat, a thought popped into his head, and it was as if someone had slapped him in the face. "Oh, brother. I forgot," he said and started rapidly rubbing the towel across his body. He still had water trickling down his back and legs as he put his underwear on and rushed into the closet. Within seconds, he had thrown on a shirt and some slacks. He didn't take time to put on socks but jumped into a pair of house slippers and raced through the bedroom.

He had forgotten about the Christmas tree lights he had left on the windowsill. *Hopefully*, he thought, *she's been too occupied with all of the scrapbooks and other memorabilia and the financial records and has not accidentally seen the bulbs.*

He reached the foot of the landing at the bottom of the stairs, but got no further before he realized he had been caught.

"John McGillicuddy," she shouted, "I hear you running through the house. Are you feeling guilty you spent half an hour in the shower?"

He raced up the stairs, and just as he slid around the corner, he collided with her in the hallway outside the bedroom.

"Ouch! That hurt! Be careful. Why did it take so long for that shower?"

Mr. McGillicuddy took a deep breath. He didn't answer the question. Instead, he said, "Oh, I'm sorry, honey. Let me get in there and finish up, and you go put the dinner on the table. I'll make sure everything else is put up, and then I will be right down."

"Oh, I know how excited you are, so I know how sad you will be that there's nothing left to do. You managed to meander around and waste enough time in that shower, and I have put everything back. I've even run the vacuum cleaner in the closet and the bedroom."

He hugged her, and with his arms stretched around her, he leaned his chin on her shoulder. She couldn't see the big smile on his face or hear the sigh of relief. He leaned back and kissed her on her left cheek. "I'm sorry. Let's go downstairs."

"Not so quick. Have you forgotten something?" She looked straight into his eyes.

He stared at her. "No, I don't think so."

"Maybe, like telling me why our mysterious strand of Christmas tree lights are lying on the bed."

Caught, he thought. "I, uh, uh ... what?"

She pulled loose from him and walked back into the bedroom. "Come in here and quit acting innocent. Just tell me why you didn't put them in the closet."

When he walked into the room and saw them, he knew that Bobby had pulled off another trick. *He must have done it when we were working in the garage.*

"That morning when we got home, I had jet lag, you remember. I was awake and wandering through the house and couldn't sleep. You were sound asleep, and so I started to unpack some things. When I saw the bulbs, I picked them up and started to put them away in the front closet, but then thought, what the heck! If we think they are so special, why not just put them in the room where Remington stays at Christmas? So, I stuck them behind the curtain on the windowsill."

He had held her right hand tightly and squeezed it while he explained. "I thought it was a good idea," he said and gave her a hug and a kiss.

"Thank you," she said. "But why did you take them off the windowsill and put them on the bed? Did you think they needed a place to sleep?"

"Uh, sure. That was it," he mumbled. "I don't know. I was upstairs this morning before you put me to work in that heated oven called a garage, and I happened to think about them. I just went in and put them on the bed. There wasn't really room on the windowsill for the strand to be stretched out anyway.

"Oh, I see." She giggled. "You just wanted them to be more comfortable."

"That's right. Now, I'm starving. Let's go eat," he said, and the two of them left the room hand in hand, he thinking, *What are those bulbs up to,* and she laughing at him.

"You mean we are really going to stay here on the bed?"

"Dimmer, why do you have to be told things three times?"

"Bobby Bright," his mom said sternly, *"you be nice to your brother."*

"Sorry, Mom. Yes, Dimmer. I think it's more comfortable, don't you? That windowsill here isn't nearly as wide as the one we were on in Spain. Being here on the bed makes it even better than in Madrid, and it means we will have been out of the closet for a whole year by the time Christmas arrives."

Actually Bobby felt a little guilty. Just a few days ago when they were leaving Spain, he believed being in a box in the closet again would be relaxing and a chance to really rest. Now he realized that was a stupid idea. This was the best of both worlds. A sun-filled room during the day, stretched out on the bed, seldom bothered because the McGillicuddys hardly ever came into their upstairs bedroom.

Bobby looked at the clock on the nightstand. It was nine o'clock, and there was still light shining through the two windows of the upstairs guestroom. *This really is pretty neat,* he thought, *having our own gigantic bed to lie on.* He wondered what Remington would think if he knew the bulbs were on the same bed that he slept in when he was here for Christmas.

His thoughts were interrupted by his mom's voice. "Bobby, you never told us what Mrs. McGillicuddy said to Mr. McGillicuddy when they were leaving the room."

"She was teasing him about putting us on the bed instead of the windowsill, and she told him that from now on it was his job to make sure and check on the bulbs every day. Then she giggled and said, 'Because that way you will know if they are comfortable.'"

3

End of Summer Cleaning

"I know I shouldn't have lied, but I just didn't want her to start teasing me about those bulbs." Mr. McGillicuddy was again talking to himself as he wheeled one of the trash receptacles to the curb.

Earlier, while enjoying the delicious pot roast dinner, he kept wondering how the bulbs had escaped the windowsill and ended up neatly draped across the bedspread. Now, as he stood by the curb, he tried to remember if maybe he had gone into the room and removed them. "That's absolutely ridiculous," he muttered and yawned. "I'm tired, but I'm not that tired. I know I didn't move them. Those bulbs have been up to something again."

Then he yawned again and a moment later, as only Mr. McGillicuddy could do, he leaned up against the trash bin, closed his eyes, and immediately dozed off to sleep.

Mrs. McGillicuddy was fiddling around in the back of the garage rearranging a few items when she realized her husband had not returned from the street. She walked to the back of the car and looked out toward the curb.

It was then she saw him and she broke into laughter. She decided to see just how long it would take for him to wake up. Even though he was at the end of the driveway, she clearly heard him snoring as the sun finally tucked beneath the horizon at 9:30 p.m.

She was still laughing as she stared at her watch, but after two minutes she decided she had enough. She opened the car door and reached inside and hit the horn three straight times.

Honk! Honk! Honk! The sound blared through the neighborhood.

Mr. McGillicuddy was literally "out on his feet." At that very moment, he was dreaming about Spain. In his dream, he was walking along the *Gran Via* in Madrid. He could hear the horns honking on the cars as they raced along one of the widest avenues in Spain. Now, as he snored and continued to dream, the horns got louder. He opened his eyes.

Honk! Honk! Honk!

He looked up the driveway, and as he did, he saw his wife shut the car door and walk out of the garage.

"What's going on, Jane?"

"Just waking you up, sleepy head. You've been standing out there, leaning on that trash bin, and sound asleep for the past two or three minutes." She pointed to her watch. "You didn't act like you were ever going to wake up, so I just helped you. Now, get in here."

They sat in the kitchen nook at the small table and stared at each other. "I don't know why you keep looking at me that way, John. It will all be fine. I am sending the letter tomorrow. First, I'm going to make a call to that light bulb factory and make sure he is still there and owns the place. If the answers are 'yes,' then I'm mailing the letter.

"It's all going to work out fine, trust me. I remember how lonely he was at that reunion. Of course, his whole life may have changed, and he may have hundreds of friends now and be very happy. But if he isn't, then it's a chance to do something good."

"I know; you're right." He tucked his head downward and stared at the floor for a moment. "I should be doing this rather than you. After all, he is my second cousin. Actually, it would be nice to get along with someone in that family."

"I just think it's the right thing to do," she said. "In fact, I look forward to his visit if he can come. I even counted the days, and there are one hundred sixteen days before we put up the Christmas trees."

4

Turkey Day Is Getting Close

The bulbs had spent the last four months in peace and quiet in the bedroom. From time to time, Mr. McGillicuddy would walk in to the room before going down the hall to work in his upstairs office, but for the most part, they were never bothered.

"I still can't believe, Aunt Glaring, that we have been so lucky."

"I know. Sometimes during the day when you fall asleep and take a nap, your mom and I will talk about how different it has been. I know your dad is right when he says, 'Enjoy this, it probably won't ever happen again.'"

Bobby's mom joined the conversation. "You know, it seemed like the days dragged by so slowly during all those years in the closet, but for me, at least, time has flown by since we've been on this bed."

Bobby looked at his mom and nodded in agreement. "I heard Mr. McGillicuddy last night talking on the phone in his office. He was telling someone that he and Mrs. McGillicuddy were going to have a quiet Thanksgiving dinner next week. But then he explained it wouldn't be that way at Christmas. He said this could be the wildest Christmas they have ever had."

"Oh, boy, Bobby," Twinkle said. "That means we will be on a new Christmas tree by next weekend. The McGillicuddys always buy their Christmas trees the day after Thanksgiving."

"You are absolutely right. You are one smart sister."

"Well, I knew that too, Bobby. Twinkle's not your only smart sister."

"Oh, Sparkle. I knew you did."

"Well, I'm your only smart brother, Bobby. I knew it too."

"Yes, but you are my only brother, Dimmer."

"Well, this is your father and I'm glad I have such a smart family."

"Well, I'm pretty smart too."

"Yes you are, Dazzling," said Bobby. "Plus, you have a different sounding voice, and you are the most beautiful bulb in our family with your mixture of green, red, and blue colors."

"Why don't we see if my daughter is as smart as she thinks she is, Bobby. I've got a question for her."

"Okay, Aunt Glaring, ask it."

"Bobby told us earlier that today is November twenty-third, and it's the birthday of Remington's mother. So, my beautiful daughter, how long is it until Thanksgiving?"

"Just four more days. Thanksgiving is the twenty-seventh day of this month."

"Very impressive, Dazzling."

"It's all because of you, Bobby. In the last year, you helped me learn to count days."

"Hey, my birthday's today, y'all. Do I get a present?"

As soon as they heard that voice, many of the bulbs began to chuckle, but the noise was quickly drowned out by the loud voice from the end of the strand. "Somebody tell Geeminy that he's got the best imagination of any bulb ever."

"Yeah, you're right, Uncle Flicker. There is no doubt about that."

"And don't forget to tell him he is the goofiest bulb in this family. Somebody tell him we don't have birthdays. We don't know what date we were born and probably never will. You know, for a member of our family who never said one word for a dozen years, you sure have said some funny things since you finally spoke to us in Madrid."

"Sometimes it takes a feller a while to get to thinking right, Flicker. But anyway, I know today is my birthday, and it's yours too, Bobby. Today is the birthday of every bulb on this strand, even if you don't want to believe me. I know a secret."

"Quiet!" Bobby shouted. "I think I hear Mr. and Mrs. McGillicuddy coming up the stairs."

"It's official, everyone." Bobby paused and said nothing. He loved to be dramatic. He waited and then the questions came from everywhere on the strand.

"Is it safe to talk?"

"Are they back downstairs?"

"What were they talking about?"

"It sounded like they were arguing."

"Yes, yes, and a little."

"Quit being mysterious. What kind of answer is that?"

"Yes, Dad, it is safe. Yes, they are back downstairs. And yes, they were squabbling a little bit." Then Bobby chuckled and sighed, "It certainly should be different."

Aunt Glaring leaned sideways and gave him a good *clink* with her shoulder. "Bobby Bright! What do you mean, different?"

"I just meant it should be another great Christmas, but there are some extra people that will make it quite different. Mr. McGillicuddy has a cousin who he's seen only once, and he is going to be here for a few days before and after Christmas. And there is another extra person because, just as they planned to do, Remington's parents brought Maria to the United States."

"I guess that means our stay on the bed is about over."

"Yes, Mom, I guess it does, but it also means we are getting ready for the reason we are here. We are about to start shining again."

It was quiet. Bobby lay near the headboard. All the bulbs were asleep, and a ray of light from the moon sneaked in to the room through the top of a windowpane.

It had been an amazing year, and now it was time for the holiday season. That meant shining, shining, and more shining. He had heard Mrs. McGillicuddy say the "Big One," their annual Christmas party for more than fifty people, was going to be later this year than ever before. It was scheduled for Sunday, December 21st. For the first time ever, Remington and his family would get to come to the big party, and there would be another new face, the much talked about distant relative of Mr. McGillicuddy.

"No doubt," he said quietly to himself, "this is going to be a very different Christmas."

But little did he know that it would be one that would bring both joy and sadness, and unfortunately, a discovery no one would ever have imagined.

5

The Day after Thanksgiving

Christmas season officially started the day after Thanksgiving. Mr. McGillicuddy always got up early and drove to the same tree lot where he had purchased Christmas trees for over twenty years. Before the day was over, both of them would be decorated.

However, before he and Mrs. McGillicuddy would begin decorating, he would test the nine strands of lights that were about to be strung throughout the tree. He always made certain that he replaced any bulbs that didn't work with new ones that shined brightly. Actually, there had been ten long cords until three years ago when the mysterious strand of bulbs had ended up on Remington's tree upstairs. Whenever Mr. McGillicuddy thought about it, he would shake his head. Some weird things had happened that day.

After the lights had been tested, he would sit down and enjoy a mug of Mrs. McGillicuddy's special apple cinnamon eggnog. Then he would return and string all of the strands neatly throughout the tree. When he was finished he would sit back down and drink one or two more mugs of the tasty drink.

By then it was time to start decorating the tree and Mrs. McGillicuddy would join him. It took a very long time to put on all of the beautiful ornaments they had accumulated during thirty plus years of marriage.

Actually, Mrs. McGillicuddy did most of the decorating because Mr. McGillicuddy couldn't stay awake long enough to help. This year had been no different than the other years. The creamy, smooth eggnog with that secret cinnamon recipe had again made him sleepy. He was now lying on the couch, snoring loudly.

Sometimes she would shout, "Wake up, John! Do you hear me? Wake up!" But today, she just smiled at him and let him sleep. After all, he had never failed since they had been married to buy their Christmas trees on the day after Thanksgiving. And he had never failed to test every strand of lights each year.

Now, as she thought about it, she couldn't help but smile and chuckle. He always tried to get out of doing any chores or any other kind of work around the house, unless he absolutely had to. So, she figured this was one thing he did right, and because of that, he deserved the nap that he was taking right now.

She sometimes was surprised that her husband was the only one whoever got sleepy after drinking her eggnog. It never made anyone else drowsy. But when that thought entered her mind, she couldn't help from smiling and chuckling once again. She said quietly, "Of course, no one drinks as many mugs as John does, and I doubt if that will ever change." *I guess I should be happy he likes it so much.*

Her thoughts were interrupted when she heard the phone ringing. As she walked to a portable phone sitting on the moon-shaped desk across the room from the tree, she saw her husband stirring as the phone rang for a third time. She was surprised to hear the voice of her daughter-in-law on the other end.

They visited for a couple of minutes, and then her son came on the line and they were chatting about the upcoming Christmas trip when she saw Mr. McGillicuddy walking into the kitchen.

As she held the phone to her ear and listened to her son outlining their travel plans to come early for Christmas, she watched Mr. McGillicuddy starting to pour the creamy liquid into a glass that was taller than the mug he had just used. *I wonder if he thinks he gets more eggnog in the glass.*

She watched him walk back into the large recreation room, where the nine-foot spruce tree sat in the corner. He stood there and admired the brilliantly colored ornaments with their many shapes and designs. The nine strands of lights winding throughout the tree were all glowing brightly and added to the beautiful scene.

A few minutes later as she continued her conversation with her son and daughter-in-law, she suddenly said, "Oh, he's back in the kitchen again." She saw him staring at her through a framed opening between the two rooms and then he started walking toward her. "Well, he was in there, but I think he's coming back in here to sit down next to me."

She paused and listened to the question on the other end of the line.

"Well, of course he has another glass with him. Nothing has changed. Anyway, I know he wants to tell both of you 'hi.' He's going to pick up the extension."

Before he lifted up the receiver, he took one more swig of his favorite holiday drink.

"Will you hurry and talk to your son before you fall asleep again?"

"Hello," he said, and then listened for only a few seconds before he broke out in laughter.

Mrs. McGillicuddy leaned over and whispered, "What is so funny?"

He covered the mouthpiece. "Oh, nothing special, just Richard giving me a lot of static for loving the 'nog.'"

She smiled, patted him on his arm, and then stood up and walked toward the kitchen but stopped to take just a moment to stare at the tree. Her husband might be a real goofball at times, but he always picked out a great tree, and after four hours of decorating it, it smelled good and looked marvelous.

From the kitchen she heard him laugh, and then he said, "Oh, yes. I'm sure she told you. It was another normal Black Friday for her and your aunts. They were out of here by five fifteen this morning to go shopping with the other crazies."

He paused and listened to his son. "Okay, I'll give her all the details." He waited for a moment and then said, "Happy day after Thanksgiving to you too, Lisa. How is my amazing daughter-in-law today? You got lots of turkey left over, or did Remington eat all of it?"

As Mrs. McGillicuddy stood near the sink thinking about the earlier shopping spree, she suddenly realized her husband had quit talking.

She looked through one of the openings between the kitchen and the recreation room. What she saw made her laugh, but she also realized what was about to happen. She rushed around the corner and into the room and shouted, "John McGillicuddy. Wake up! You're about to spill that eggnog."

She reached for the glass, and he looked up at her with surprise. "What are you yelling for? Lisa and I are talking. I can't hear her. You are making too much noise."

"Give me that phone. You actually fell asleep while talking to your daughter-in-law. Go take a nap, my goofball husband." She picked up the receiver, which was lying on the desk. "Is anybody still on the other end?" Then, she heard a voice. "You won't believe it, Lisa."

She listened before replying. "Well, of course you couldn't figure out why he hadn't said anything to you. Now you know. He was too busy sleeping. It's a miracle he didn't snore like he normally does. Listen, I have to tell you something. We are going to have someone staying here with us when you, Richard, Remington, and Maria come for Christmas. I need to give you some details."

"How was your little nap, dear?"

Mr. McGillicuddy stretched and yawned, and his long arms fell across the back of the wide leather couch, which sat in front of a very tall and wide television set in the middle of the room.

"Wonderful. I feel good. You aren't still talking to the kids?"

She laughed. "No, that would be a very long conversation. You were asleep for two hours."

"What? You've got to be kidding?"

"No," she said. "Buying the tree, putting up the tree, testing all those bulbs, helping me decorate it, and then having to drink my eggnog is enough for any man, no matter what his age, to flake out and fall asleep."

"Shoot! I thought I was going to get to talk to Remington. How is our little ten-year-old doing?"

"He's so excited about coming for Christmas again, and since we told him last month that we might have an even bigger surprise this year, he said he had a big calendar hanging on his bedroom wall, and every night, he marks another day off of his countdown to December twenty-first.

"I told Richard and Lisa all the details about your cousin coming and that he will be here with us. You know, we are going to be crowded with Maria also here."

"What did they say about Robert?" Mr. McGillicuddy asked. "Were they surprised?"

"Yes, quite a bit actually. I warned them he was a little bit strange. Maybe I shouldn't have said that. I gave them a few more details, and they did remember us talking about him a few years ago."

Mr. McGillicuddy stretched his long arms and then jumped to his feet. However, he didn't move. He just stood there, and then without warning, flopped back down on the couch.

"Come here and sit next to me. I've been wondering about something."

As she sat, she asked, "So, what's on your mind?"

He turned and looked at her before he draped his right arm over her shoulder. He gave her a quick hug and smiled. "I just wonder what it will be like seeing my second cousin again. You know, we were probably only together, the three of us, for no more than thirty minutes. I can't believe I ever agreed to go to that family reunion way back then. We barely knew anyone there. I was so uncomfortable that day, but I felt even worse for Robert. It was awful the way everyone treated him. I even heard some people whispering that he was the 'Canadian-American' in the family, as if that was some kind of a crime.

"Believe me, I know how he feels. In fact"—he smiled and patted his wife's shoulder—"those long-lost family members are probably all saying the same about me."

"What's that?"

"I'm sure they all think that I'm the other strange member of the family."

"They may be right, dear."

6
It Was Unbelievable

The whole town was talking. Those who found out told their best friends or family, and in every case, the person they told said, "Are you sure you aren't kidding me? You mean Old Man McGillicuddy is going somewhere for Christmas?"

Then those people would tell others, and in Calumet, Saskatchewan, where only 2,713 people lived, it took only three days. By December 15th, everyone in town knew. They all wanted to believe the rumor was true, but they couldn't.

But you know what? It was.

Robert "Old Bob" McGillicuddy only had three real friends, and the reason they were his friends was pretty darn evident. His best friend, if you could really call him that, was his banker. The Busy Lights and Bulbs factory placed all of their money in the Calumet Bank of Saskatchewan. There was plenty of that money, too, because Robert McGillicuddy's company was the largest Christmas tree light bulb factory in the world.

Old Bob's second best friend was his stockbroker who had sold him all of his stocks and bonds for over twenty-five years. Every year the stockbroker sent very expensive birthday and Christmas gifts, but Old Bob never used them. The stockbroker didn't care as long as he kept selling stocks.

Then, there was friend number three. He was what people liked to call a "money management counselor." That meant he found ways to make the money Old Bob gave him make even more money. What money Old Bob didn't give his stockbroker, he gave to his third friend, and that was still a lot of money.

Old Bob had actually seen his third friend—once. He came all the way from New York City to the closest airport to the factory. He had a limousine waiting to drive him to the tiny town. When he arrived, it took them only five minutes to sign all of the necessary documents. The "money man" explained to him that they were "the most important papers you will ever sign." As soon as the signature of Old Bob was dry on the paper, the money man, without even taking time to have a cup of coffee or a soft drink, jumped into his limousine and was driven back to the airport.

They had never seen each other since.

Those were Robert McGillicuddy's best friends, and they were his only friends.

It wasn't that people really disliked him. People never had a chance to like him. He was in his office at five o'clock in the morning. At six o'clock, he was on the production floor checking all of the giant belts that carried the bulbs to the assembly area, where they were placed on strands. He examined every belt and every giant machine on the huge factory floor every morning.

At seven o'clock, he was in the bookkeeper's office making sure every order had been filled properly, and more importantly, that the bills for the thousands of bulbs made daily had been sent out immediately. He liked that done quickly because it meant the money that people owed him would be paid to him quicker.

And of course, his only three friends liked that very much.

At eight o'clock, he watched every worker enter the factory, and though he never really scowled at anyone, he had never been known to smile since the day he had opened the business over twenty-six years ago. Of course, then it was just a tiny building with only two rooms and three employees.

One of those employees had been his personal secretary, Debbie. She had been with him since the first day, and although he hardly ever smiled at her, she knew deep down in her heart that he was a good man, even though he was a sad and very lonely man.

As the business grew quickly into the world's largest bulb factory, it meant Old Bob McGillicuddy had to spend even more time overseeing all of the departments of his huge business. Each day was filled with many, many duties as he watched thousands of bulbs joined together on long strands and boxed for shipment around the world. He had to be sure that every order was filled properly, and of course the best part was sending out the bills to collect the money. Then, after watching every employee leave in the late afternoon, he would spend a few more hours in his office or on the factory floor. The one thing he did always manage to do was get home by midnight.

The clock read eleven thirty, and he was ready to leave for the evening. He took an extra moment to lean back in his chair and gaze through the wide office window that overlooked the biggest production room in the factory. He was the owner of a company that had 1,000 employees, twenty production rooms, and more money than even his only three friends could count. But he was also one of the loneliest and saddest people on earth.

The calendar on his desk read December 15th. All of the last-minute orders for Christmas had been placed and filled. It would not be hectic for the next few days like it had been for the past month.

Maybe that was why his thoughts wandered back to the surprise letter he had received this past summer. It was a letter that would change his life forever.

Over the past few days, more and more people had heard the rumor, and they continued to shake their heads in disbelief. Most of them refused to believe that Old Bob was leaving town for Christmas. Some of the townspeople even claimed they had heard he was actually going to spend Christmas with relatives.

"Unbelievable! Unbelievable! Unbelievable!" That one word must have already been repeated at least ten thousand times during the past week.

And despite all the rumors, there wasn't a single person who could truthfully say they even knew Old Bob had any relatives. That's why the news was unbelievable.

It was Friday, December 19th, and tomorrow, the townsfolk of the tiny little hamlet of Calumet, which was covered with two feet of snow and preparing to celebrate Christmas, were going to see a miracle. The man, who ran the company that provided jobs for almost everyone in town, was leaving to spend Christmas away from his beloved factory.

And if that news wasn't enough to keep everyone gossiping, yesterday Old Bob had added even more spice to this mysterious story.

He had called Debbie, his long-time secretary, into his office just moments before he was to deliver a speech to all of the workers. He spent five minutes with her giving her some very specific details about his plans and making sure she had written down everything he said and knew how to follow his instructions. When he was finished, she opened the door; and as she was leaving his office, she turned to him and asked, "Mr. McGillicuddy, are you sure you are feeling all right?"

When he didn't answer, she closed the door behind her. Less than a minute later, he opened it and walked over to her desk. He leaned down and looked her directly in the face. "Oh, yes, Debbie. I'm feeling better than I have ever felt and tell Kenneth, that husband of yours I'm buying both of you that motorcycle you have always wanted."

He turned away quickly and walked down the hall. He left too soon, and he didn't see the shocked look on her face, nor did he hear her say, "I think he has lost his mind."

When he reached the door to the walkway that over-looked the production floor, he stopped for a moment and said quietly, "Are these people ever in for a big surprise." And then he did something no one had ever seen him do.

He smiled.

He peered down at all of the employees staring up at him and proclaimed that for the first time in the history of the Busy Lights and Bulbs factory, the workers would have a full week of vacation beginning two days before Christmas.

The crowd below cheered loudly until Old Bob raised his hands in the air to prompt them to be quiet. Then he announced that the vacation was actually longer than a week. "Don't show up until January second."

The crowd cheered even louder as people looked at each other in utter disbelief.

"What's gotten in to him?"

"He's not the same man."

"I can't believe it."

The comments came from all corners of the factory. Some people still refused to believe until he shocked them even more. He raised his hands for a final time and proclaimed, "And all of you will be paid for your holiday vacation, too."

It was just unbelievable.

7

A Strange Visitor at the McGillicuddy's

Bobby heard the garage door open as he lay at the front of the tiny tree in the guestroom. Every time Bobby heard that sound, he would think of the many times he had overheard Mrs. McGillicuddy say, "John, that door is so noisy. Get it fixed."

But of course, he never had. He always had an excuse when she told him to call a repairman. So, as soon as Bobby Bright heard the squeaking and grinding of the door's cables, he knew the stranger had arrived from the airport.

"*You know what this means,*" he shouted to the other bulbs on the strand. "*This long-lost relative is going to be the next person we make happy when we shine brightly tomorrow night at the 'Big One.'*"

Bobby listened to the noise downstairs, and occasionally, he understood a few words. The McGillicuddys were walking through the house showing the visitor their home. When they were at the foot of the stairs in the foyer,

Bobby overheard Mr. McGillicuddy tell the man about the tornado that had hit the McGillicuddy's house over two and a half years ago.

Then Bobby heard something that really surprised him but also made him proud. Although he didn't hear all of the conversation, he heard enough to know that Mr. McGillicuddy had explained to the visitor how Mrs. McGillicuddy had been saved from dying by a strand of brightly lit Christmas tree lights packed tightly against her leg.

"Will you tell us again who this man is?"

"Not now, Mom," he whispered. *"It will have to wait. I hear them coming up the stairs, but I will tell you this: the man said the story sounded unbelievable, but since his company made Christmas tree light bulbs, he wanted to see what these bulbs looked like."*

"Robert, I hope you don't mind sleeping upstairs. If it wasn't Christmas, you could stay in this guestroom," Mrs. McGillicuddy said and pointed to the doorway. Old Bob glanced to his left as he reached the top of the stairs and saw a room with a tiny Christmas tree on a table and the foot of a tall bed that stood at least a couple of feet above the floor.

They walked to the opposite end of the hall, and as they started into the room, Mr. McGillicuddy hurried to join them. "Hey, that's a good bed here in my office, Robert."

"Whenever Jane gets angry at me, I come up here and pull out that sleeper bed, and it's very comfortable."

"Oh, John, quit trying to be funny." She chuckled and looked at their newly arrived guest, who appeared uncertain if he should laugh, or if he really understood.

"Come on, Robert, John is only kidding." She looked at him again, and when she smiled, the smallest bit of a smile crept across his face.

"I can already tell I'm going to like it here." It was some of the first words he had said since he had arrived. "Would both of you do me a favor?"

"Sure, I guess," Mr. McGillicuddy mumbled.

"Oh, John. Of course we will," Mrs. McGillicuddy quickly answered. "What is it?"

"Would both of you call me 'Bob'? At the factory everyone always says 'Mr. McGillicuddy' when they speak to me. Of course, I know that behind my back, everyone in town only knows me as 'Old Bob.'"

"Well, we certainly aren't going to call you old, but we will call you 'Bob,'" said Mrs. McGillicuddy, and she smiled once more at him.

"And you know what, cousin? We are going to have a good time while you are here. We want you to enjoy Christmas."

Before Bob could answer, Mr. McGillicuddy continued, "And believe me, this really is a good bed. Plus, you will enjoy our grandson, Remington. He will be sleeping in the bedroom we passed at the top of the stairs.

"If you need to use my computer to check e-mail or anything else, feel free to do so. Now, let's get this bed set up for you, and then we'll leave you alone."

Mr. McGillicuddy took the cushions off the sofa and pulled the hidden bed free. "I can't believe that at three o'clock in the morning you drove through a snowstorm for a hundred and fifty miles to the airport. Then to think your plane to Chicago was delayed three more hours. What did you say it was, twelve hours to get here? You must be exhausted."

Old Bob nodded his head.

Mrs. McGillicuddy interrupted her husband. "So, relax for a couple of hours. By then, our son, Richard, his wife, Lisa, and our grandson, Remington, and their nanny should be here. All of you are in for a big treat tomorrow afternoon and evening. We have a huge party every year for about fifty people, and we call it the 'Big One.' Each of you will get to be a part of it for the first time."

Bob smiled, but a confused look remained on his face. "Uh, I sort of remember something about a party when we talked on the phone last week."

Mr. McGillicuddy put a long fluffy pillow on the bed and said, "Yes, I mentioned it, but enough about that for now."

Bob stared at his long-lost cousin for a moment and then softly said, "Thanks. John. I'll take a quick nap for an hour."

"You sleep as long as you want," added Mrs. McGillicuddy. "We'll have a late supper when you wake up."

Mr. McGillicuddy fiddled with his mug.

"You must not be feeling well, John."

"Why, dear?"

"I've never seen you take this long to drink a cup of my eggnog."

"Maybe I'm trying to stay awake in case we ever get to eat dinner. Shouldn't the kids and Remington be here by now?"

"Be patient!" She looked at her watch. "It was an hour and a half ago when Richard called. I told you he said it was snowing pretty heavily. It was nearly dark at that time, so it's going to take them longer than it normally would."

"Well, I just hope they are careful." He stood up, swallowed the last of his eggnog, walked quickly to the refrigerator, opened the door, grabbed the large pitcher, and refilled the mug.

"You know, John, you could save some room for supper."

"I've got plenty of room in my stomach. I'm starved. It's already seven fifteen."

"Oh, quit being so dramatic. Have you forgotten Spain? We never ate before nine o'clock at night. You're acting like it is midnight."

She started to say something else but stopped and put a finger to her mouth. "Shhh! I hear him coming."

"Hello," he said quietly, as he walked into the kitchen.

"Hi. I bet you are starved," Mrs. McGillicuddy said and smiled. "Did you get anything to eat on the plane? They charge you for everything nowadays. We found that out both times we flew to Spain in the last year."

"Oh," he said softly. "I thought you had already eaten."

"My goodness, Robert, uh ... I mean, Bob. Did you think we would invite you here and then just sit down and eat while you were asleep?"

"Well, maybe not. I did have a great nap, Jane. I guess I slept more than two hours."

"Well, hopefully we won't starve you much longer," Mr. McGillicuddy interjected. "We are still waiting for Remington and his folks to get here. In fact, I'm getting a little worried with that snow starting to accumulate. It looks like there are three or four inches outside, and most of it has fallen since we picked you up at the airport.

"You know, Jane," he continued, "maybe we should just go ahead and eat, and the kids can eat when they get here. What do you think of that idea, my long-lost cousin?"

"Uh … uh … sure," he said timidly. "Sure, let's eat."

"All right, you two hungry guys, I'll get everything on the table." But just as she said it, the doorbell rang.

8

A Time to Meet New Friends and Family

Mr. McGillicuddy opened the wooden front door and looked through the storm door. He started laughing immediately and so did Mrs. McGillicuddy when she peeked around her husband and saw who was staring at them through the glass. Standing there, with snow on his face, on his cap, and all over the front of his coat and pants, was their ten-year-old grandson.

"Hurry, Grandpa! Open the door. I'm freezing."

"What happened to you?" he said and pushed the storm door open.

"Come in here, right now." Mrs. McGillicuddy stepped around her husband and hugged her grandson.

"I slipped and fell," Remington said and pulled loose from her. "You can hug me later, Grandma. You're going to get snow all over you, plus I'm hungry. Can I get something to eat right now?"

"Oh, don't be silly," she said. "A little snow won't hurt me. Of course, you can get something to eat. I've got all kinds of stuff in the kitchen."

"Good, because I am starved. We didn't stop the last four hours."

"Well I've got my homemade chicken noodle soup, some fried chicken, and then you can have a piece of blueberry pie. But first, get out of the cold. Get in here where it is warm." She pulled him into the foyer.

"Well, let me have some of that snow and a big hug to go with it too." Mr. McGillicuddy bent over and lifted his grandson into the air. "Whoa, buddy. You're even heavier than you were this summer in Spain."

Remington gave his grandfather a huge squeeze with his two arms and then jerked his head away and said, "I hear Rocket."

The big, golden haired, long-time member of the McGillicuddy family was barking with excitement.

"The whole neighborhood can hear Rocket right now," laughed Mr. McGillicuddy and set his grandson's feet back down on to the floor. He's in the garage. Go tell him 'hi' and give him a couple of treats to eat. You'll be surprised. We'll help your mom and dad get the luggage."

"Okay, but then I've got to get upstairs and see Bobby and the bulbs."

Remington raced away, and the moment he opened the door, Rocket really started barking. Remington stepped down from the hallway into the garage and then turned around and shouted, "Wow, Grandpa! You've made Rocket a real palace out here. He's got a cool place to live."

Before he could say anything Mrs. McGillicuddy shouted back to Remington, "It was your grandpa's idea when he was cleaning out the garage after we got back from Spain. He really enjoyed cleaning it up."

Just then the front door opened again, and Remington's mom and dad walked into the foyer brushing snow off their clothes. Mrs. McGillicuddy grabbed each of them and gave them a big hug. Mr. McGillicuddy did the same, and then Mrs. McGillicuddy started crying as she did every year. "Don't any of you say a word. I can cry if I want to when I am happy to see my family."

She stepped away from her son and daughter-in-law and looked through the glass door. Thick flakes of snow were falling, lit by the front porch light. "Oh, my gosh, Lisa! Where is Maria?"

"She's in the car, waiting."

"Waiting for what?"

Lisa looked at her mother-in-law. "She is a very special lady. She said she wouldn't come inside until we had all greeted each other and been together for a few minutes. We tried to tell her that was silly, but she insisted."

"Well, enough of that. She will be freezing out there. Did you keep the engine running so she would stay warm?"

Before her son could answer, she had already opened the door and stomped outside.

"Jane, be careful. Don't you want your coat and your boots?"

Mrs. McGillicuddy paid no attention as she stepped gingerly through the small drifts of snow in the driveway. Then, she opened the door of the SUV. "Oh, Maria. It's so wonderful to see you. Get in here right now. Don't you know you are as much family as all of us are?"

Mrs. McGillicuddy put her arms around her and helped her out of the car, and she was still hugging her when they walked in the foyer. "Now, you should feel much warmer."

"Jane, give the poor woman a chance to breathe. Welcome to our home, Maria."

"*Con mucho gusto, señor,*" Maria said to Mr. McGillicuddy.

"Well, it's a pleasure to meet and see you again too, Maria."

"Wow, Dad. You really understood her. You mean you actually remembered something I taught you."

Mr. McGillicuddy looked at his son. "No not really." He smiled. "But I remembered what Maria taught me."

He took her hand and said, "Come on in the house, Maria."

"Thank you, *señor*. But you say, *Pasa en mi casa.*"

"Oh, don't try teaching me too much Spanish." He laughed again. "Anyway, one more time, welcome to our home."

Everyone else had already taken their gloves and coats off, so Mr. McGillicuddy started collecting them so he could hang them in the foyer closet. At that moment the hallway door opened, and Remington raced back inside from the garage and headed through the crowd in the foyer.

"Grandpa. You did a great job. Rocket's got a neat place to live out there, and his own heater, too. I'll show you Rocket later, Maria," he said, and brushed in between her and Mrs. McGillicuddy. "Right now...I'm going upstairs to see Bobby and the bulbs!" and he dashed up the stairs. However, he ran only about four steps before he turned and ran back down.

"What's wrong?"

"Oh, nothing, Grandma. I want Maria to come with me to see the bulbs."

"Oh, Remington McGillicuddy! Give Maria a chance to take a tour of our house; plus, I have someone I want her to meet. The bulbs can wait."

She stood there looking confused. Remington's dad looked at his son and said, "You go back upstairs. She will come up in a few minutes." And then, he said to Maria, "*No te preocupes. Mas tarde, puedes visitar con Remington y las bombillas magica.*"

"Richard, talk English; and Mom, would you please introduce us to this poor man standing in the dining room and wondering what's going on?"

Mrs. McGillicuddy started to motion for Old Bob to come into the room, but before she had a chance Remington jumped off the stairwell landing and came rushing into his grandmother's arms. "I've changed my mind. I'm hungry. I want to eat now."

"You can have something to eat after we introduce our guest."

"No. I'm too hungry."

"Well, I've heard everything now," said Mr. McGillicuddy. "My grandson chooses food over his magical bulb. I guess you don't like, Bobby, anymore?"

"Oh, Grandpa, of course I like him. I love him. But, I am hungry. The bulbs can wait. My stomach can't."

Everyone started laughing, and then Mrs. McGillicuddy said, "Come on, Bob."

Robert McGillicuddy had been standing a few feet away in the next room, and he looked astonished at all the hugging and kissing and chattering that was taking place in front of him. This was a scene he was not used to seeing, and for a brief moment he realized just how lonely his life was.

He was so interested in just watching everyone, he didn't hear Mrs. McGillicuddy at first. He was still just looking in astonishment at all the talking and hugging when he suddenly saw her motion with her hands to come into the foyer. "Bob. I want everyone to meet you."

He paused a couple more seconds before he finally took a few steps forward and the introductions began. Lisa hugged Bob. He got a slap on the back from Richard. With a very formal handshake, Remington said, "Nice to meet you," and Maria also shook his hand and said, "A pleasure, *señor*, uh, I mean, sir."

"Well, it's nice to meet all of you. I haven't known your grandparents very long, Remington." And then he paused as if he needed to think what to say. "Well, I guess I've known them for a few years, but I've only seen them once until I got here just a few hours ago. I know this: even in the short time I've been here, they sure like to talk about you."

Remington smiled. "Well, that's nice to know because I talk about them a lot."

Everyone laughed and Mrs. McGillicuddy said, "John, you and Richard go bring the luggage inside. I'm going to go finish preparing dinner. Everyone must be starved. Remington, it won't take but about twenty minutes and we'll eat."

"Oh, Grandma, I can't wait that long. How about at least some soup?"

"Remington, you can wait to eat." His mom smiled. "I can't believe you're not upstairs seeing if that bulb, Bobby, is doing something magical."

"It's not funny, Mom, laughing about it."

"I'm not laughing. You've convinced me he's magical. It's just strange you haven't rushed up there and left us all alone down here."

"Well, it's just that I saw the bulbs almost all year in Spain. You know that." He turned away from his mother and watched his grandmother walking down the short hallway and into the kitchen. "Okay, I'll wait to eat," he hollered from the foyer. Then he turned and looked at his grandfather. "Is my tree really larger than last year? Is it the best one yet?"

"I think it's the best one," said Mr. McGillicuddy. "One thing for sure, it is full of branches, and it is definitely prettier than that scrawny one you had in Madrid."

"Come on, Maria." Remington waved from the stairs. "You can come with me."

His nanny looked at Remington's mom as if she needed approval to go upstairs in a stranger's home. But before Lisa said anything, Mrs. McGillicuddy hollered from the kitchen, "Maria, you do whatever you want. *Mi casa es su casa.*"

"Wow, Grandma! That was good."

Mrs. McGillicuddy peeked her head around the corner and smiled. "I've been doing some practicing. I may try to say some other things in Spanish while you are here."

Across the room, a wide smile covered the face of Maria. She was looking into the eyes of the woman who had changed her life with the gift of a pair of dresses when she was a beaten and worn-down, old, homeless woman in Madrid. Jane McGillicuddy was her hero and always would be. She clapped her hands together and applauded. "*Buen dicho, señora. Buen dicho.*"

Remington had already reached the second floor, but he yelled back down the stairwell, "She said that you speak very well, Grandma, and you do. Congratulations!"

In the corner of the foyer, Old Bob again stood and watched in wonderment. *So this is what family is all about.* Then he did something he rarely did. He smiled.

9

A Reunion and Strange Feelings

"There they are," said Remington.

"Oh, *Dios mio!*" exclaimed Maria. "The tree. It is beautiful. It is more than beautiful, Remington. It is…uh, Remington, what is that word in English? It is like *precioso* in Spanish."

"Let me think. I know. Don't help me."

Maria laughed. "Remington, it is me need help. The word I try to remember is like *pretty* but means *magnifico* or more beautiful."

"You mean, 'gorgeous'?"

"That ees eet. Thank you. The tree, eet ees gorgeous."

"Well, what about the bulbs? Aren't they beautiful? There is Bobby right in front like he always is."

"How many years you know that scary bulb?"

"He is not scary. He is just full of magical powers. You know that, and you know he can even say a few English words."

"Don't remind me, Remington. Eeet ees, eet ees…oh, I get so angry at me when I don't remember words."

"Your English is better than my Spanish. What is the word?"

"That's what I want to know. In Spanish, we say, *extraño.*"

"You mean, *strange?*"

"Eeet ees even more than 'strange,'" she answered.

Remington put his right index finger to his lips and looked toward the ceiling.

"You look like school professor," she said.

"I'm thinking. I ... I ... I remember. Do you mean, 'weird'?"

"That is it. These bulbs, and that blue one are weird and scary."

Remington noticed Maria had pronounced *is it* correctly. She only said *ees eet* when she was excited. "Not *scary*, Maria; these bulbs are beautiful. Did you know that it is tradition in the McGillicuddy family to turn the tree lights on every night at six o'clock and keep them on until eleven o'clock?"

"What that you say?"

"Tradition."

"You mean it is tradition like it is at your house."

"Exactly. It was like that when dad was a little boy. Hey, you want to see my dad's old bedroom and all his basketball trophies?"

"Sure. I had *trofeos* when I was young too."

"You? What did you win trophies for?"

"*Futbol.*"

"Girls don't play football." Remington scowled and looked at her like he didn't believe her.

"Why you look at me like that? Are you angry?"

He started laughing. "Just kidding you, but I don't believe you."

"Oh, yes. I great girl *futbol* player when I was in what you call high school."

"Maria, you didn't play football. Not for real, did you?"

"Not American football, Remington. Everyone else's football."

"Oh, you mean soccer."

"Yes, soccer. But it is correctly called *futbol* or football."

Maria and Remington had barely left the room when the chattering started.

"Tell us now, Bobby."

"What did they say?"

"Why did Remington leave so quickly?"

"Whoa! I can't answer everybody at once. Let me talk." And then, he told them.

"But why does she think we are weird, Bobby? You know I like Maria. She was careful with us in Spain when she would clean Remington's bedroom, and you told me she

really believed she had heard you squeak out some words in human language. Why does she think we are weird?"

"Mom. Be real. She saw me flying through the air when Remington was lost in Madrid. She knew what happened that night. She knows the police, and the other Spaniards she told the story to, never believed her. But she knows we have powers."

"No," his mom interrupted, "you are the only one with the magical powers."

"Well, whatever. She still knows we are different, and to her, that is weird. But I think she is still frightened by us."

Just then, he heard voices at the foot of the stairway. "Be quiet! Somebody is coming back upstairs."

"I can't wait for you to see my tree, Mr. McGillicuddy. I know you will like my bulbs. They are really different and unique."

"That's a pretty big word for a ten-year-old, Remington."

"How did you know I was ten?"

"I told you. Your grandparents have talked a lot about you, especially when they were driving me here from the airport. They told me you are a very smart young man."

"Thank you, but I don't know about that."

Remington walked into the room but stopped in the doorway and turned around with his arms stretched out and the palms of his hands upward. "Here they are the most beautiful bulbs in the world and on my very own tree."

"Wow, you are right, Remington. They are beautiful, and I know quite a bit about Christmas tree lights."

They were sitting side by side on the bed. For over fifteen minutes Remington had been talking and telling stories about his special blue bulb. He was right in the middle of another tale when he suddenly stopped and jumped up. "I want Maria to come back up here and be with us. I'm going to get her right now."

"Good," said Old Bob, and he smiled.

Old Bob sat on the side of the bed and stared at the bulbs. Since Remington had left the room, he had felt very strange. "In fact," he said quietly, "I felt strange the moment we walked into the room."

He chuckled to himself as he thought about the many things Remington swore the bulbs had done. Every story was greater than the next one, especially the one about Jane being saved from a tornado two years ago.

"He does have an imagination," he whispered.

As he waited for Remington to return, he stared at the tree. His eyes followed the strand of lights as it stretched through the branches. He had the strangest feeling as he looked at the bulbs. There was just something different about them.

"This is ridiculous. I see thousands of bulbs a day, but these really are—he hesitated as if trying to think of the word—gorgeous, that's what they are." He remembered Remington saying that Maria had used that same word to describe the bulbs.

He closed his eyes for a moment. It had only been half an hour since he had been introduced to Remington's nanny, but he thought the word *gorgeous* perfectly described her. He opened his eyes and looked at the tree again. When he did, he felt a shiver run through his body. He looked down at his arms and saw goose bumps.

"Why are you sitting there staring at the tree?" Remington said, as he walked back into the bedroom.

Old Bob turned his head quickly. He hadn't heard Remington coming up the stairs. He didn't answer. He sat very still. Then he turned around and looked back at the tree.

"Are you all right, Old Bob? Mom said it was okay to call you that." When there was no answer, he paused a few seconds and then asked again, "Are you all right?"

"Uh. ... sure. ... sure, I'm fine."

"You weren't moving or saying anything. In fact, you look pale."

"Pale? How do you know what pale looks like?"

There was a gruffness to Old Bob's voice that Remington had not heard before. "Are you mad at me?"

He stared at Remington and didn't answer.

Remington didn't like the way he was being looked at. Just as he started to ask again, Old Bob answered. "I'm sorry, Remington. No, I'm not angry with you. Let's go downstairs."

"But don't you want to stay and enjoy the bulbs? Maybe if you look at them closer, you can tell if they were made at your factory."

"You know about my factory?"

"Yeah, mom told me it is the biggest in the world. I guess that would mean there is a chance they were made there, right?"

"Oh, I don't think there is any doubt. I am nearly certain they were made at my factory." Then another cold shiver ran down the back of his spine. It was like the one he had felt just minutes ago. And once more, he could see the goose bumps on his arms. "Let's get out of here. It must be time to eat. It's late, and I am starving."

"That was marvelous, Jane. I can't believe you had so much food for what you said was going to be just a 'small' dinner."

"Well, I'm glad you enjoyed it. I'm sorry it took so long. Besides there really wasn't that much. I didn't want to serve you a big meal because we're having our annual Christmas party tomorrow night. I will cook a couple of dishes, but almost everything is catered by our two favorite restaurants, the Deep Fork Grill and Interurban."

"I remember you telling me about that party last week when you called to make sure I was coming. Is it really okay for me to be at the party?"

"What are you talking about, Robert?" Mr. McGillicuddy asked. "Why in the world wouldn't you be invited? You are our guest and staying here in our house. Plus, you are family. All those other people are either close friends or people I have done a lot of business with."

"How many people are you talking about?"

"We always have more than fifty, so it is pretty crowded, but it is a lot of fun."

"What do you do at this party? Does it last very long?"

"I know the answer to that. Grandma, remember when you phoned us last week, and you told me about the games? Since I'm the only kid at the party, do I get to play them, or are they grown-up games?"

"Hey, Mom, we are looking forward to this too. I told Lisa that I haven't been to the Big One since I went to college."

"Hey, Daddy! I bet I can beat you at some of the games, if there are any I can play. Are there, Grandma?"

"Yes, dear. You can't play the word game, it will be too difficult; but you can play the dart game, the golf putting game, and the toilet paper toss."

"The what?"

Lisa put down her fork and looked across the table at her mother-in-law. "What game?"

"I will let your father-in-law explain. He talked me into this goofy game two years ago."

"It's simple, and whether you want to admit it or not, Jane, everyone loved it. In fact, some of the guys who will be here tomorrow night told me they had been practicing this week throwing toilet paper rolls. It's an easy game and fun. Everyone who loses thinks it's only luck. Those who win know it is skill."

She started to turn and go back into the kitchen, but stopped and said to everyone listening, "Well, let me just say this. If I won, it would definitely be luck. Now go ahead and tell them how to play it."

"It is simple. You stand at the top of the stairs and throw the rolls down to the landing. There is a large dinner plate setting there. If a roll stands up straight or lies up against the plate, you get from one to three points. It is easy and fun."

Mr. McGillicuddy looked across the table. There was no response until finally Old Bob broke the silence. "Sounds good to me, although I sure didn't think I was taking my first Christmas trip so I could throw toilet paper down some stairs."

Everyone began to laugh, and they were still laughing when Mrs. McGillicuddy walked back in to the room with two big pitchers in her hand.

"Oh, boy, look at that," said Mr. McGillicuddy.

Maria had hardly spoken during dinner. She had eaten quietly while the others at the table had visited. She understood some of the conversation, but often times got lost when everyone talked at the same time. But when she saw the pitchers, she said, "Señora, ees that your favorite nog of the egg? I remember you telling me about it in Madrid last summer."

Remington laughed. "You said that wrong."

"I did? What wrong with nog of egg?"

Everyone at the table smiled, and in a gentle voice, Mrs. McGillicuddy explained. "Don't worry, Maria. You just got the word backward. It is eggnog."

"Oh! Eggnog," she said slowly.

"And is it ever good. Quick, all of you pass me your glasses, and I will pour you some. Normally, John pours himself a glass and never thinks to pour me one. At least, not until he has emptied the first glass and refilled it at least once."

"Oh, Jane. That's not true."

"Yes, it is," said Remington's dad. "We all know the truth. We've seen you snoring and sleeping after drinking too much of Mom's eggnog. That apple cinnamon recipe gets to you every time."

Mr. McGillicuddy poured his cousin the first glass and waited for Old Bob to try it. It didn't take long for his reaction.

"Wow! What's that taste?"

"It's what Richard just said. It's my special apple cinnamon recipe. I will warn you. It may make you drowsy. One glass is enough to make John sleepy, and by the time he has had three glasses, he's ready for a nap."

"Not true," said Mr. McGillicuddy. "It takes five glasses before I am sleepy."

As laughter filled the room, Mr. McGillicuddy filled every glass. Then, he made a toast to the most marvelous Christmas ever and "to our two special guests."

Maria looked across the table and saw the man smiling at her. She tilted her head down and looked at the colorful Christmas tablecloth. A moment later when she looked back up, he was still staring and smiling. As she smiled back, the clock chimed for the first of eleven times.

"Oh, my goodness. We've got to get to sleep," Mrs. McGillicuddy ordered. "It's a big day tomorrow. After we get back from church, all of you will have to pitch in and help me. There will be a lot to do before the party starts at four o'clock."

"So, everybody drink up. When you are finished, Remington, you and Bob can go ahead to bed. The rest of us will get the table cleared and the dishes put in the dishwasher. Then, let's get some sleep."

The sky was dimly lit with a quarter moon, but a sliver of brightness peeked through one of the windows in the second-floor office. Robert "Old Bob" McGillicuddy's eyes were wide open. After telling everyone good night at the dinner table, he had come upstairs. Now, as he lay there on the pullout bed, he looked across the room at a large window. Above it was a much smaller window, and through it, he saw a few more moonbeams that had managed to stream their way into the room. The strips of moonlight sprayed across the digital screen of a clock sitting on the desk. It read 1:30 a.m.

He had been in bed for nearly two hours, and he was pretty sure he had never fallen asleep. He did remember that when he had first gotten in bed, he had been lying there only a few minutes when he heard a noise. Remington was asleep and his dad was carrying him up the stairs, but as they entered the bedroom, Remington mumbled that he wanted his Christmas tree lights to remain turned on while he was sleeping. He had gotten his wish.

Through the open door, he could see the soft glow of Remington's strand of friends.

What a feeling! Christmas tree lights! It's kind of nice to know that I make so many people happy.

Old Bob rolled over on his left side for what must have been the twentieth time. He just couldn't sleep. Something was on his mind and had been since the moment Remington had shown him the tiny tree and the strand of lights.

"It just won't go away," he mumbled quietly to himself. "I simply can't quit thinking about it."

He rolled back over on his right side, and as he did, he again looked down the hallway. The brightness of the tree lights enabled him to see into the darkened bedroom.

"I've made my mind up. I'm doing it, no matter what." Quietly getting out of bed, he put on his house slippers and a robe and tiptoed down the hall. Inside the room Remington was lying on his back with the bed covers tucked under his chin, and there was the slightest sound of snoring. Old Bob smiled and bent down to look at the shining lights on the tree.

Immediately, he experienced that same cold chill that had run down his spine before dinner just a few hours earlier. He looked very close at the blue bulb in front of the tree, and then he peered deeper into the branches where he saw a bulb with mixed colors.

He reached in and touched the red, blue, green, and yellow bulb, but for less than a second. He jerked his hand back. He had burnt his fingers. The bulbs were really hot, and he thought how dumb he was not to have figured that out.

He straightened back up and continued to look at the tree. Within the past two hours, he had dismissed this thought from his mind twice. But this time, he couldn't. The worst moment in his life had happened fourteen years ago. Two days before Thanksgiving, a terrible accident destroyed almost every bulb in the factory.

As he envisioned the moment again, he heard Remington. When he turned around, he saw him roll over on his side and mumble something in his sleep.

That was enough. He hustled out of the room and walked down the hall. He crawled back into bed. He wasn't sure he could possibly go back to sleep. There was a nagging thought in his mind, and it wasn't going to go away. He would try to check and see if his suspicion was true, but he would do so when the lights were turned off and there was no one in Remington's bedroom.

10

The Big One

Mr. and Mrs. McGillicuddy's special Christmas party—the Big One—had been held on a Sunday evening in December for more than twenty years. Each party had one thing in common. There was always plenty of delicious food, marvelous desserts, and some crazy and goofy games that everyone enjoyed playing. Mr. McGillicuddy always gave away expensive prizes to the winners, and sometimes they included special, all-expense-paid trips to a famous resort. It was the party the McGillicuddy's friends and business associates always talked about.

Remington's dad remembered the first time they had ever given one. It was his last year in middle school, which had been twenty-four years ago.

"Well, Daddy, I'm even younger than you were when you went to your first Big One," said Remington as father and son waited at the front door to greet the next arriving guests.

"Yes, you are, and I haven't been to one since my last year of college. That's at least fifteen years ago, so we should be happy your grandma and grandpa decided to wait until just four days before Christmas."

"Well, I'm sure glad. This is going to be fun."

"You can thank Grandpa's second cousin, Robert, for that."

"You mean Old Bob, Daddy?"

"Yes." His dad chuckled. "I mean him.

"Well, anyway, when your grandparents called him earlier this year to invite him to come for Christmas, they decided they would have their party later than they ever had so he could attend."

"And thanks to him, I get to play like I am a doorman." Just then, the doorbell rang again.

"*There's the doorbell again. Do you hear it?*"

"*Well, of course we hear it,*" bellowed Uncle Flicker from the middle of the tree. "*Do you think we are deaf?*"

"*No, Uncle Flicker.*" Bobby started laughing. "*I don't think you are deaf. I was just getting ready to say that it won't be long before there are enough guests here to start coming upstairs and playing games. Remember, two of the games are played up here. So, I guess we better start turning up the juice and shine as bright as we can.*"

"I can't wait," said Aunt Glaring. "You know, Bobby, as much as I enjoyed our amazing Christmas in Spain last year, and as much as I enjoyed the 'Spanish Big One' for Remington's classmates from the embassy school, I missed the faces of the people back here. The two years we have been up here on Remington's trees, we have actually gotten to shine for people and see them react."

"I know," interrupted Bobby's mom. "It was never like that on the big tree downstairs the first nine years we were here."

"How could it have been?" Bobby's dad joined the conversation. "No one ever saw us because we were always hidden at the back of the tree."

"I hope that goofy old couple who has been here both years comes and looks at us again."

"Why, Aunt Glaring?"

"Because each time the husband has gotten right down in our faces and said the same thing, 'I never saw such bright lights in my life.' He has that big old grin and two of his teeth are missing, and he makes me laugh."

"Quiet! I hear Mr. McGillicuddy," Bobby interrupted. "He's bringing some of the guests upstairs."

A woman walked into the room followed by her husband and two other couples.

"I said it last year and I'll say it again. Those lights are beautiful. They just seem to shine brighter than any I have ever seen." She turned to her husband and after a quick sip from her glass, added, "And Jane still makes the best eggnog in the world. I don't know what she does but it is delicious."

"It sure is," he said, and they clinked the two glasses together in a toast to each other. Then he bent over and leaned in close to the tree. "Just look at them. I've never seen such bright lights in my life." He grinned, and some eggnog dripped between two missing front teeth.

In the corner of Remington's bedroom, standing alone as he watched each of the guests, was Old Bob. So many people who had walked into the room had remarked that they thought the Christmas tree lights were the brightest they had ever seen, and after a lifetime of checking and testing Christmas tree lights, he agreed. They were the brightest. He was proud they had been made at his factory, a fact he had confirmed only a few minutes ago after the first guests had arrived.

He had slipped away from the crowd, hurried upstairs, and checked some of the bulbs on the strand. It took only five minutes to verify something he was almost certain of. There was no question that the bulbs were from the Busy Lights and Bulbs Factory.

Now, as he stood there thinking about his discovery, another couple walked into the room. They had won an award earlier in the evening for being the first persons at the party. The man waved and smiled. "How did you do in that crazy toilet paper toss, sir?"

Old Bob ducked his head and paused for a moment, but before he could answer, another couple walked in, and the four people started talking. The man and his wife were no longer interested in him, and less than a minute later, the two couples left the room and he was alone again. He was glad. He didn't want to admit he hadn't scored a point in the game.

He looked into his cup, and it was nearly empty. *That Jane can certainly make good eggnog.* He swallowed the rest of the creamy drink and, seconds later, decided it was time to go downstairs and see what else was going on at the party. As he turned to leave the room, he caught a glimpse of himself in the mirror on the wall and then something behind him.

He couldn't believe it, and in his shock he accidentally dropped the cup. He was lucky because it missed the wooden floor and landed on the rug unbroken. With all the noise in the hallway, no one heard.

He quickly picked the cup up. When he stood up, he turned his head and again saw himself in the mirror. He was standing there with his mouth wide open and a shocked look on his face.

He had every reason to look that way. He had just seen that blue bulb move back and forth on the tree limb.

"Are you out of your mind, Bobby Bright?" his mom scolded him. "What did you think you were doing? You made him drop his cup, and if anyone had seen him, they would have thought he was ill or something was wrong with him."

"Hey, Mom, he's a McGillicuddy. He should know we are different and have magical powers."

"Quit trying to be funny, Bobby. He doesn't know anything, and he doesn't need to. Don't you ever think of doing that again!"

"All right, I am sorry."

"Hey, I have an idea, Bobby."

"What is that, my smart little brother?"

"You know you told us that man makes Christmas tree light bulbs?"

"Yes, I told you that, but he does more than just make them. I heard him tell Remington that he is the owner of the world's largest Christmas tree light bulb factory. I think he knew exactly what he was looking for, even before he started feeling around the tree and touching all of us. He wanted to see if we had been made at his factory."

"What was he looking for?" asked Dimmer.

Bobby raised his voice so all the bulbs could hear. "What he was looking for he found on—"

"Me!" hollered Energizer. "He found it on me. He pulled me up off the branch, and I thought he was going to unscrew me from my pod, but he saw something."

"He saw something humans call a stamp," Bobby explained. "There is a code word used for bulbs made in that factory. He now knows we came from there."

"Well, he didn't act like I had any secret word on me," Uncle Flicker's loud voice rattled throughout the tree.

"There's a reason. You didn't have one. They only mark a few bulbs as they go down the conveyor belt. But they mark enough that there is always at least one on each strand.

"Dazzling, you are the bulb he was most interested in because of your red, blue, green, and yellow colors mixed together. I heard him mumbling that he was certain you would have a stamp. He said it even before he pulled you up in the air and looked. Even though he expected to find it, he acted frightened when he saw it."

"Why do you think I scared him, Bobby?"

"I wish I knew."

They had no idea that they would get the answer in just a few minutes, and it would be the biggest shock in their life.

Meanwhile outside the room the party was coming to a finish and Mr. McGillicuddy had given prizes to winners of four of the five games. He stood at the foot of the stairs and prepared to announce the final winner.

Bobby listened carefully and then there was a loud cheer. All of the guests began clapping their hands. Above the sound of the applause there was one familiar voice laughing.

"What's going on? In all these thirteen years I know I've never heard Mr. McGillicuddy laugh any louder."

Bobby twisted to his right and looked at his dad, who was smiling. "I agree and he had a good reason."

Bobby always enjoyed being dramatic, and so he paused and waited even though he knew why everyone was applauding. Sparkle was impatient and wanted to know now.

"Will you please hurry up and tell us. Why did Mr. McGillicuddy laugh so hard?"

"Patience, my dear sister. Mr. Mac took an extra long time in introducing the winner of the toilet paper toss because she was probably the most unlikely person in the whole house that could win."

Again Bobby paused.

"What the heck is going on with you? You just get on with it. We are not interested in that drama stuff you do and makin' us wait like a bunch of old puppy dogs. Tell us right now."

Bobby twisted and looked behind him and then downward to a lower branch where Geeminy was grinning at him. "*Wow!*" Bobby yelled. "*You just keep getting ornerier, now that you finally learned to say something after all these years.*"

"*Thatta boy, Geeminy. Let him know what you think.*"

"*Thanks a bunch, Blinker, for cheerin' me on, old buddy. Now, you get on with that story.*"

"*I know we are all tired after the party, and I know none of us have ever shined any brighter and longer than we did tonight. But I think you will be happy to know the winner of the toilet paper toss was Maria.*"

The bulbs cheered. They all remembered how nice Maria had treated them in Spain and how careful she was when she dusted them at least three times a week.

"*You see, Mr. McGillicuddy was laughing because Maria closed her eyes each time she threw and then squealed when she looked down the stairs and saw each of the rolls sitting up on the plate.*"

"*I am so happy for her. She was so wonderful to us earlier this year,*" Bobby's mom said.

"*What was her score?*"

"*I'm glad you asked, Dazzling. The score was just like what you used to think you were.*" Bobby chuckled softly.

"*What is that supposed to mean? Explain yourself.*"

"*Remember when you used to think you were perfect?*"

"*Well, that was before I finally decided to be nice.*"

"*Yes, it was. Anyway, Maria's score was perfect. Each of the three toilet paper rolls she threw down to the*" *bottom of the steps landed straight up on the plate. It was the only perfect nine-point score."*

Before they could cheer again, Bobby heard Remington and the old man talking at the foot of the steps downstairs.

11

The Accident Remembered

The two of them sat next to each other on the side of the bed. Remington's feet were on the top step of the two-step stool that allowed him to climb into the high bed. Old Bob's feet were stretched out in front of him and nearly touched the closet door.

"You know, I thought we might have a little chat about some things."

"Sounds good to me. At least we're not having to help clean up all of that mess downstairs."

Old Bob turned to Remington and smiled. "Well, I offered to do something, but Maria told me she was going to help Mrs. McGillicuddy and that I should go with you and see that you get ready for bed."

"You know what? I think you must really like Maria. You sure spent a lot of time with her tonight. *¿Habla Español?*"

Remington waited for a couple of seconds, but when Old Bob just kept staring at him, Remington said, "Just wondered if you spoke some Spanish?"

"Oh, no! But she was very nice, and she spoke English good enough. We had a nice visit, mostly about you. She told me how she had been saved by your family, had moved in with all of you in Madrid, and became your nanny."

"I saw you hold her hand for a moment, didn't I?" Remington grinned.

Old Bob had never been married and probably had never had more than a couple of girlfriends in his entire life. He just didn't have time for anyone. He worked every day of the week. When he heard Remington, he couldn't help but blush.

"Why are you turning red in the face?"

"Oh, nothing. Now forget about Maria. I have something important to tell you. I'm going to stand over here at the foot of the bed, and I want you to sit there and pay very close attention to what I am going to say.

"Remember how you have spent the last two days telling me about these lights on your tree and that special blue one in the middle you call Bobby?"

Remington nodded.

"Well, I have been thinking about these stories, and I have been sneaking in here and looking at the bulbs." He started to say something else, but Remington interrupted.

"You have been sneaking upstairs and looking at my bulbs. Why?"

"It's part of what I am trying to tell you. These bulbs definitely came from my factory. Let me show you something."

"Can I get out of bed? You told me to sit here."

"Of course. Come here."

Remington jumped down from the bed, and by the time he reached the tree, Old Bob was holding on to a bulb near the bottom. It was red, blue, green, and yellow.

"See this bulb," he said and pulled the strand up where Remington could see.

"Sure. I've seen that bulb a bunch of times. It's easy to see with all of those different colors. I always wondered why it was there. I remember the first year the bulbs were on my tree. I saw it and I couldn't believe it even lit up, because it was so different from the others."

"Well, there is nothing wrong with it, just that it is strange-looking. However, the bulb never should have been put on the strand. It should have been thrown away."

"How did it happen?"

"Well, most likely, there was some kind of an accident or the machine didn't work right. When a bulb goes through the coloring process, it passes beneath a machine that lightly sprays each bulb a different color. When this bulb passed, red must have been the next color of paint, but somehow, the machine failed to switch colors properly. As you can see, little drips of blue, green, and yellow must have spurted from the nozzle and fell to each side.

"So what does that have to do with what you are going to tell me?"

"Be patient. This is important. So, listen carefully. You are about to hear something no one else in the world knows about."

The sound of Bulbese echoed throughout the tree.

"*You mean we really were the only bulbs who survived?*"

"*I knew there was an accident, but I didn't think we were the only bulbs that weren't broken.*"

"*How lucky were we?*"

"*All these years, and we never knew.*"

Finally, Bobby shouted, "*Hey, there is more. Let me finish the story.*"

His mom very seldom raised her voice. But she made sure she could be heard this time. "*Let Bobby talk. I am nervous about all of this. I want to know what happened, and I want to know all of the facts now.*"

"Like I told you, we were the only bulbs to survive the conveyor belt accident that day, but there is more to the story. There was a man who was in charge of the conveyor belt and he was—"

"*What's a conveyor belt?*"

"*Yeah, what's a conveyor belt?*"

He twisted slightly so he could see both of his sisters and answered, *"It's the big belt that carries the bulbs from position to position. According to Old Bob, the bulbs travel on that belt from the moment they are made. They even take a side trip to another smaller belt, which takes them to the paint machines. That's where each of us got a different color."*

"Well, then what happened to me?" asked Dazzling.

"He talked about that, too, and in fact, you may be the main reason we now know the truth."

"What do you mean by that?"

"Just give me time to finish and quit interrupting me."

"Bobby Bright!" His mom turned and frowned at him. *"Your sisters and Dazzling each have a right to ask questions. So does anyone else if they don't understand."*

"Yes, Mom. Sorry, Twinkle and Sparkle. Sorry, Dazzling. Anyway, this is how Old Bob explained the story to Remington. He said the belt operator fell asleep for just a moment, right after he had eaten his lunch. Apparently, his head fell forward, and he actually hit his nose on the belt. That woke him up, and the first thing he saw were bulbs flying all over the main room of the factory. Do any of you remember that?"

Aunt Glaring turned and looked at him with disbelief. *"You have to be kidding. That was a long time ago."*

"I know. I just wondered. Well, anyway, according to what Remington was told, except for us, every bulb on

the main floor of the factory was destroyed. As they flew off the long belt, they hit other pieces of machinery, the floor, and even the ceiling. They were smashed into tiny pieces. It was a mess."

Bobby paused and waited. He expected to hear questions. But there was only silence. He glanced to his right and saw tears on the face of his mom. When he looked the other way, he also saw tears on Aunt Glaring's face. He leaned forward and looked down among the branches at other members of his family. There was the sound of quiet sobbing. The bulbs were speechless and shocked. They all realized how lucky they had been on that fateful day.

He continued. "As soon as he realized what had happened, the conveyor belt operator grabbed for the big switch that controlled the speed of the belt. But the moment he pulled the switch, electricity shot from the generator box, and the operator later told Old Bob that he started slipping on the rolling bulbs on the floor, and when he grabbed for the belt and touched it, the belt screeched to an abrupt stop."

Bobby paused, and when he did, the questions followed.

"What happened?"

"Go on, Bobby. Tell us what happened."

"Did the belt operator get hurt?"

This time, he waited politely before continuing.

12

The Happy Accident

"The man running the conveyor belt didn't get hurt, but the bulbs did. When Old Bob heard all of the noise and rushed down to the main production floor, there were employees from many other sections of the factory already there. They were laughing and pointing at the belt operator."

Bobby paused to recall what he had heard Old Bob tell Remington, but just as he started to continue, his father interrupted.

"Some of you think my memory is not as good as it was because I was stepped on over two years ago. I haven't spoken very much since then, but I have listened and been patient. Most of my memory has returned. I think I know why the other employees were laughing at the belt operator. It was because of you, wasn't it, Bobby? Am I right?"

"I love you, Dad. You are smart, and you are right."

"What is he talking about?"

"He saw something that day, Mom. It is something that I have known and often wondered about. It is my oldest memory."

Bobby's dad started laughing.

His wife stared at him. "*What is so funny?*"

"Yeah, Daddy, tell us," Bobby's two sisters chirped. "What is so funny?"

"Your brother got his magical powers the moment that electricity shot from the generator box. And we got our powers to speak in our own language because the few of us that weren't broken also received smaller shocks of electricity. But Bobby was the one nearest the box, and he received so much that it gave him the superpowers that he has had all these years. It gave him the power to not only speak in our wonderful Bulbese language but to also understand human language. And of course, as he grew older, the power that he had received that day increased more and more. As the years went by, he became so strong he was able to do all the wonderful things he has accomplished in recent years. You see, there is a reason our Bobby Bright is the world's most amazing Christmas tree light bulb." And then Bobby's dad raised his voice and looked directly into his son's face.

"I can't understand humans like you can, so I don't know what the old man was telling Remington, but I am still pretty sure I know why all of those employees were laughing and pointing at the belt operator."

"Well, go ahead. You've been right so far. Take a guess."

"Oh, it isn't a guess. It's the first memory I ever had. I was lying on the floor. There were a few bulbs, like me, that weren't broken, and we were scattered underneath the belt. I looked up, and I saw this giant. Of course, now I know it was the belt operator, and when I looked at him, even then before all of these wonderful powers had soaked in to our bodies, I knew it was funny."

When his dad paused and didn't say anything else, Bobby smiled. His dad could also be dramatic.

"Oh, please go on. Tell us what happened."

"Okay, Mom. Do you want Dad or me to finish?"

"I don't care. Just tell us."

His dad decided. "Go ahead, finish the story."

"The reason all of the employees laughed"—he made sure he was talking loud enough to be heard—"was because I was stuck in the nose of the belt operator."

"No! Are you serious? My brother was inside a nose of a human."

Bobby peered back through the branches at Dimmer and nodded. "Yep. Right inside one of his nostrils."

And at that moment the tree began to shake, and snickering, chuckling, giggling, and boisterous laughter filled the room. Amidst all of the noise the questions were repeated over and over. "You mean you were stuck in his nose? How did you get in his nose?" Each time they were repeated there was more laughter.

"Oh, no! Is that ever funny. You were really in his nose?"

And above all of the laughter, Bobby Bright admitted to his family, "It is true. That is the moment I was born. In fact, that is the moment all of us were born."

"Okay, I brushed my teeth," said Remington, as he hurried back into the bedroom. "Now finish the story, please, Old Bob."

"By the time I got to the main production room, there were workers from all parts of the factory there. I shooed them back to where they had come from, and I got very angry with Dale, the belt operator. I told him to send the bulbs that weren't broken to the strand machine. I had no idea how many there were, but I knew all the others had been destroyed.

"I never even saw the bulb in his nose. Some of my employees told me about it later. There was nothing else I could do, and so I closed the factory and sent the workers home. It took us two days to clean everything up and get the machinery running smoothly again.

"I never forgave, Dale. Even though there were only four weeks until Christmas and it was our busiest time at the factory, I punished him. I sent him home, and he didn't get paid for three weeks. Only when his wife came and begged me did I give him his job back, but at lower wages than before."

It was late and Remington was tired, but his eyes were wide open. He wondered if he would be able to fall asleep after hearing the details of what had happened on that historic day. But he also knew his mom would be coming up the stairs any minute to make sure he was in bed. "Hurry and finish the story."

"Just give me a minute." Old Bob stood up and walked out of the room. Remington saw him wipe the side of his face with the back of his hand. He followed him into the bathroom.

"Is there something wrong?" Remington saw him grab a tissue and wipe his eyes.

"No, I'm okay." But then Old Bob began to sob, and when he turned around, the tears streamed down his cheeks.

"Here, let me get you some more tissues." Remington reached around him and pulled a handful of blue tissues from the box. "Here, take them. Are you sure you are okay?"

Old Bob took the tissues in his hand and wiped both cheeks. He even blew his nose, and even though Remington felt sorry for him, he started laughing.

"What's so funny?"

"You sounded like a foghorn on a ship."

Then it was Old Bob's turn to laugh. "Yeah, I probably did."

"Are you going to tell me why you were crying?" Remington pulled on his new friend's right hand. "Come on back in the bedroom and finish the story."

"Not much left to say," he answered, as they walked back into the room. They sat down next to each other on the corner of the four-poster bed.

"The bulbs went on their way. They were placed on a strand, and all the employees were so afraid of me that no one at the strand machine said anything about the bulb that had been painted too many colors. It should never have left the factory. It should have been thrown away."

"Well, I'm glad you didn't because Dazzling would never have made people smile when she shined."

"Dazzling? What are you talking about?"

"Well, I have secrets too. Earlier this year, I taught Bobby some human words. He squeaked a few of them, but he also taught me some Bulbese. That is what my grandpa calls their language when he is making a joke."

"But who is Dazzling?"

"Oh, yeah. Well, when I was teaching Bobby earlier this year, I was just getting ready to screw him back in his socket. He squeaked a word, and I thought it sounded like *dazzling*. When I asked him what that word meant, he rolled along the windowsill, where the strand was lying, and he touched the bulb with all the colors. It's the same one we were talking about earlier. So, I think her name is Dazzling, and who knows, maybe all the bulbs have names."

"I will say this for you, Remington, you have convinced me these bulbs are magical, but no one has an imagination like you."

"Remington McGillicuddy, are you in that bed?"

They both heard her stomping up the stairs.

"Hurry, tell me. Why did you cry?"

"Because I did the wrong thing to poor old Dale. When I get home, I'm going to give him three weeks pay, plus fifteen years of interest on the money he lost."

Remington remembered his mom had mentioned that word *interest* when he had opened his first savings account at the bank. He was pretty certain that if Old Bob gave the belt operator fifteen years of interest, it would make him a very happy man.

"Why would you do that?"

"Because I know now I was the one who made the mistake. I will tell you about it later."

"So there you are, still awake," said Remington's mom, just seconds after he had scrambled back in to bed.

Old Bob tilted his head downward and looked at the floor. Then he raised it ever so slightly and looked into her face. "It's my fault. We were having too much fun talking about Christmas tree light bulbs and my factory."

Standing between the two of them, she couldn't really be too upset. She looked at her son who smiled and said, "It was really interesting. Maybe I will tell you a neat story someday."

"Well, not tonight. It's okay, though. You two look like you have enjoyed talking."

"Oh, we had a great time. Now would you two let me go to sleep?"

They both laughed and left the room.

"Thanks for not turning off the bulbs. I love looking at them before I fall asleep."

"Oh, you're welcome, sweetheart," she said, as Old Bob joined her, and they walked down the stairs.

He lay still until he was sure they were at the back of the house. He jumped out of bed and raced to the tree. He bent down and looked at the blue bulb. "Bobby, I love you and all the bulbs. Always remember that, but I am going to do something to make someone else happy. The bad news is it will make you and me sad."

The clock on the nightstand read 1:45 a.m.

Bobby was wide-awake. He could hear Old Bob snoring at the other end of the hallway. He laughed quietly. "It must run in the family. He snores like Mr. McGillicuddy."

But this is not a laughing matter, he thought. I didn't like the sound of what Remington said.

13

Christmas Day

In past Christmases, Remington had always wanted to unwrap his presents on Christmas Eve. He was content to only open his gifts from Santa Claus on Christmas morning. But this year, it was different.

"I know he is only about three months from turning eleven years old," said Mr. McGillicuddy, "but even so, I thought he would still want to open those presents last night. He didn't even argue when we told him we wanted Bob and Maria to experience a Christmas morning filled with lots of gifts being opened."

"Well, maybe it's part of him growing up. Anyway, I know one thing for certain. It is sad and unbelievable that Bob has gone all these years without spending Christmas day with anyone. I hope we can have him come again in the future."

"Me, too, and I think he might have found a reason. Did you see how he and Maria spent most of yesterday together?"

"Oh, yes. I noticed. It's almost as surprising as seeing you here in the kitchen with me at six thirty on Christmas morning. I am in shock."

"Just trying to be a good husband and help prepare the turkey."

"That first cup of eggnog wouldn't have anything to do with it, would it?"

"Well, maybe a little." He lifted the cup to his lips, tilted his head back, and swallowed the last of the eggnog. "Boy, that is good. I think I will get some more." He started to open the refrigerator door but paused when he saw Maria walking into the kitchen.

"Good morning, Maria." Mrs. McGillicuddy waved at Remington's nanny then she turned back to her husband. "John, no more eggnog until you have helped me get the turkey in the oven."

"*Buenas dias, señora y señor, y Feliz Navidad.*"

Mr. McGillicuddy stood by the open refrigerator. "And a Merry Christmas to you, too."

"And from me also," said Mrs. McGillicuddy. Aren't you in a wonderful mood? Look at you! You are already dressed for dinner, and I am in my bathrobe."

"*No te preocupes.* I am sorry. In English, I say 'don't worry.' You are fine. I still can help in my good clothes."

Mrs. McGillicuddy laughed. "Why did you get dressed up so early? We are going to be sitting around on the floor opening Christmas presents."

"Oh, it okay. I want to look for him, good."

"What? What are you talking about?"

"Sorry, Meester McGillicuddy. I just mean, I dress right for Bob."

"Ah-hah! We were right, dear."

"You right about what, *señor?*"

"Well, I think," Mrs. McGillicuddy interrupted, "that you like John's cousin."

"Yes, I do, but I don't like when everyone call him Old Bob. Me no think he old."

Mrs. McGilliuddy laughed. "I can tell that."

"Here, let me help with the *pavo.*"

"The what?"

"Sorry, *señor.* You move away. Let us work with the turkey."

"Sure thing. No problem." Mr. McGillicuddy quickly opened the refrigerator door.

Even though Remington was downstairs and no one would be coming upstairs until much later, Bobby and his family still enjoyed Christmas Day. They shined brightly as if someone was in the room enjoying their brilliant glow. They enjoyed hearing the sounds of laughter and music from downstairs. Christmas carols echoed throughout the house the entire day. It was a McGillicuddy tradition.

When dinner was served in early afternoon, the dining room was close enough to the bottom of the stairs that Bobby could hear bits and pieces of the conversation at the table.

"Mrs. McGillicuddy just told Old Bob that he is trying to make up for all those Christmas meals he missed before. She told him it was okay to have a fourth helping of mashed potatoes and turkey. Everyone has been laughing at him, but like Mr. McGillicuddy said, 'It still hasn't kept him from continuing to eat.'

"Somebody just asked him, if he had room for any dessert."

"Well, does he? What did he say?"

The voice came from the right side of the tree, and Bobby peered through the branches and saw Energizer. "I'm not sure, but I think he said 'yes.'"

"Maybe he is too busy eating to talk." Aunt Glaring leaned over and touched Bobby and laughed.

"You are probably right. Anyway, they are all having fun, and since they are, why don't we also have some fun?"

"I'm not hungry."

There was a smattering of chuckles throughout the tree.

Bobby smiled for a second and then said loudly, "Are you still trying to be funny?"

"You be nice to Flash."

Bobby looked at his mom and nodded his head. "Ok!" And then he raised his voice and said, "Hey, listen up all of you. Why don't we practice shining so we will be brighter than we have ever been when Remington comes up here after dinner?"

Bobby's mom nodded back to her son. "And I know the best way to do that, let's sing our very own song."

And that's what they did, spending the early part of the afternoon singing and singing. Had there not been so much noise downstairs, the McGillicuddy family might have thought there was a television set turned on upstairs.

> We're gonna shine all Christmas season.
> We're gonna shine every night.
> We're gonna shine, shine, shine,
> And be very, very bright.
> Now today is Christmas Day,
> That means we'll shine all day long.
> And when the night finally arrives,
> We will still be shining strong.

Finally the bulbs were tired of singing and wanted to rest. It was now very quiet. Bobby tried to relax too, but he was a little uneasy, and he felt sad. He looked at the digital clock. He was surprised. It was four o'clock and Remington had not been back upstairs to see the bulbs since he had left to go unwrap Christmas gifts this morning. In the past three years, twice here and last year in Spain, Remington had opened his presents and then rushed back up to be with the bulbs. Then after dinner he had hurried back up to see them shine brightly.

Bobby didn't know what it was, but as much as he loved Remington, and knew his human buddy loved him, he had a feeling for the past four days that something was wrong. It seemed like Remington didn't spend as much time with him and his family as in the past. He thought of their good times together over the past three years, and as his mind wandered, filled with happy memories, he felt himself getting sleepy. He leaned sideways and his eyes closed. When he re-opened them he saw the clock across the room. 4:25 p.m. He was surprised that he had been daydreaming so long. *I wonder where he is.*

The answer came just a few seconds later when he heard steps on the staircase and lots of laughter and everyone chattering away at the same time.

The six adults had two sheets of paper in their hands. Remington had been in charge of passing out the Christmas songs.

Old Bob was impressed. "I think it is a wonderful idea you had, for all of us to come up here in your room and sing these Christmas carols. That's exactly how it should be and it makes sense too."

Remington frowned and looked at his new friend. "What do you mean by that?"

"Because those brightly shining bulbs on your tree came from my factory."

"Are you serious?" Mrs. McGillicuddy seemed surprised. "How can you tell?"

"Well, if you look closely at two or three of the bulbs, they have a very small stamp near the base. Sometimes you can barely see it when a bulb is screwed in to the socket."

"You mean you checked to see?"

"Oh, yes, John. I was so interested in Remington's stories about the bulbs and how strange and different they were that I started examining them and found some had our factory's logo stamped on them. Like I said, it is very small and can hardly be seen."

"I see Remington has got you believing in the magical bulbs like the rest of us," Remington's mom said and walked over next to the tree. "I suppose he has you believing this little guy right here"—she stuck her finger up against the blue bulb at the front of the tree—"is Mr. Magical."

Remington tugged on Old Bob's arm and looked up at him. "Don't worry; Mom wants to sound like she still doesn't quite believe all the stories. But, like I told you, she does. We all do."

"Well, you and I know the real truth about those magical powers, don't we?"

"I thought we weren't supposed to talk about it."

Mr. McGillicuddy looked at Remington. "What have you and Bob been up to?"

"Oh, it's our secret. Now, are we going to sing Christmas carols, or not?"

"Let's go," said Mrs. McGillicuddy, and everyone began to sing "Silent Night."

It was a wonderful Christmas. By night time, the McGillicuddy family and their guests had opened marvelous gifts, eaten delicious food, sang many, many beautiful Christmas carols, and had experienced a day together that they would all remember.

"That's what Christmas should always be, every year," said Mrs. McGillicuddy to her husband. "A day to remember. I hope everyone had a wonderful time."

Down the hallway, their son and lovely daughter-in-law were also getting ready for bed. They stood side by side staring out the window and looking at a light covering of snow on the ground. Richard looked at Lisa. "It was truly a special day."

"Yes, it was. Good food, gifts, love, and friendship."

"And from the looks of things, a new friendship between Maria and Old Bob."

On a pullout couch in the large recreation room, even with the lights off, Maria could easily see the outline of the giant Christmas tree in the corner of the room. She couldn't believe how blessed she was. Just one year ago, she had spent Christmas on the downtown streets of Madrid, begging for food, and living in a cardboard box. Now she had a real family again, and as tears gathered in her eyes, she thought, *And a man I believe I could like very much.*

He lay on his back and stared at the ceiling. A sliver of moonlight peeked through the top of the wooden blinds that covered the front window in Mr. McGillicuddy's office.

Today had been Robert McGillicuddy's greatest Christmas ever, and he would never forget it. He could only hope that his cousin, John, would invite him again. He had learned in four quick days how wonderful it was to have a family. He had never enjoyed anything like this in his entire life. He was certain he would start being a different boss when he returned to the Busy Lights and Bulbs Factory.

14
A Surprise for Old Bob

Remington stared at the bright bulbs shining on the tree. He had begged his mom to please not come back up and turn them off later.

"It's Christmas. Please let them shine all night." She had looked at him with a strange look on her face, and Remington wondered if she had any idea about what he was about to do.

During the past fifteen minutes he lay awake and heard the snoring of Old Bob at the other end of the hall. He smiled. He had heard lots of that during the past few evenings.

However, within the past few minutes, there had been no noise. Remington lay there trying to decide if he should do it. Finally, he made his mind up. He got out of bed and tiptoed down the hallway to the office. The door was partially open. He peeked his head into the room, but he still couldn't see the sleeper bed, and he pushed the door open a little wider.

"Who is it? Who's there? What's going on?"

Remington almost jumped out of his pajamas. "Oh, you scared me. I'm sorry, but I didn't hear you snoring so I thought you were awake."

"Well, I am, but you frightened me." Old Bob sat up in the pullout bed. "The door was moving, and I couldn't see anybody."

Remington started to laugh, and then his old friend did too. "Can you come back to my room with me?"

"Sure, I guess. What's going on? Is your mom going to be angry that you are out of bed?"

"Not if we are quiet."

"What do you have planned?"

"I just want to tell you something in front of my Christmas tree."

"You can't tell me here?" he whispered.

"No. Come on. It's important."

As they held hands and walked down the hall together, each of them could see the tiny tree through the doorway. The lights were glowing very, very brightly.

"Those lights on your tree sure are pretty. They look great from here."

"They sure do, and you know what? They have to be the brightest bulbs in the world."

"Maybe that's because they come from a great factory, or at least a great one when the boss isn't making mistakes and fouling things up."

Remington turned and looked up into the face of his friend who he had met only a few days ago. "It's okay. We all make mistakes."

They entered the room together, and Remington walked to the bed and crawled up on it and sat on the bedspread.

Old Bob leaned against the doorframe and watched his young friend. *He is one great kid. I wonder what's on his mind.*

"Come here and sit down beside me, please. I have to tell you something because we will be leaving tomorrow around noon."

"I know. Your dad offered to take me to the airport since it's on the way."

"Oh, good," said Remington. "It means I can see them for a few more minutes."

He looked at Remington, who was standing in front of him. What do you mean? See who?"

"That's what I want to tell you. I will be eleven years old in just over three months. I know about Santa Claus and the Easter Bunny, and I am getting older."

Robert McGillicuddy had never really been around children, and so he had no idea what was happening or where the conversation was going. But he had learned a lot in four days about being around a family, and he decided to only listen.

"I love these Christmas tree lights, and I know that Bobby is really magical, and I believe they can speak in their own language. When I asked Bobby that earlier this year in Spain, he answered me the way he does when he means 'yes.' He tilted himself forward and backward…"

As Remington continued talking, Old Bob looked down at the floor. Even though he was listening to his young friend, he kept thinking, *I want to believe Remington, but sometimes the boy's imagination makes it pretty tough to do. Even so, I am sure that the electricity from that generator box fourteen years ago affected the bulbs in some way.*

"So, what do you think?"

"What did you just say? He looked up into Remington's face. I was daydreaming, sorry."

"I just said I want you to take the bulbs back to Canada and keep them at your factory so you will remember how special they are."

"What? Why would you want me to do that? They really belong to your grandparents, don't they?"

Remington didn't answer.

"Well, even if they really are yours, don't you think if you believe you are getting too old for a tree in your bedroom, then they should go back to your grandparents? They could put them on their big tree downstairs each year. You told me that was where they used to be, anyway."

Remington stared at him for a moment before he spoke.

"These bulbs are different because of what happened at your factory. If it hadn't have been for the accident, the bulbs would have been like all others. But they aren't, and because of that, I have had a chance to enjoy all of them, but especially Bobby. I've told you all of the stories about the miraculous things he did and how he saved me and my grandparents. They are very, very special, and I will never forget them, but I still think you should take them."

Old Bob stood up from where he was sitting on the edge of the bed. He put his hands on Remington's shoulders and slid him off the bed. Then he picked him up and held him in his arms. "But that blue bulb is still your friend."

"Yes, he is, and he always will be. I won't forget him as I get older, but all of the bulbs would be perfect in your office. You told me it overlooks the main floor of the factory. They would always mean something to you. Only you know the truth about their magical powers and how the accident caused everything to happen."

"It's hard to believe you are only ten years old." He patted Remington on the back and let him down onto the floor.

"I'm not," he quickly said. "I am almost eleven."

"Well, you are acting and sounding like someone much older. This is a wonderful thing you want to do. Have you told your grandparents?"

"No, but I will. They love me, and they must love you too. I know they are very glad they invited you here, and they want you to come back."

Old Bob started laughing. "Well, that is good news to my ears because I want to come back. And, I want to come visit you. But what does that have to do with your plan?"

"My grandparents will be happy if I am happy. And I will be happy if you have the bulbs. Plus, my mom will be the happiest. So, tomorrow, take them with you. I will even keep them in my lap until we reach the airport. It will be tough, but I want you to have them."

Remington's head was facedown. He had been looking at the floor when he had said those final words. Now, he coughed and lifted up his head. When he did, he realized both he and Old Bob had the same problem. Tears were rolling down the cheeks of both of them.

"There will never be another Christmas like this for me," Old Bob said, and he started to cry some more.

Remington took two quick steps forward and hugged him.

"You know, I just thought of something."

"What?" Remington asked.

"I can hardly wait to show them to the conveyor belt operator when I get back. Dale will be awfully happy when he hears what happened, and especially when I admit that part of the accident could have been my fault because I didn't check the conveyor belt the night before."

"See, I told you this was the right thing to do."

"You are a very, very special, bright young boy with a wonderful heart. Thank you. I will cherish them forever."

"You're welcome."

15
Good-Bye Forever

While no one probably knows for sure, it would certainly make sense that Christmas tree light bulbs that are crying can't shine very brightly.

After Old Bob had tucked him in to bed, Remington had laid awake for a few minutes. But, he finally fell asleep, and he wasn't sure what time it was when he suddenly awoke and sat straight up. He looked across the room. Something was strange. It was Bobby. He was barely shining. He slipped out of bed and hurried to the tree and lifted up the front of the strand. He put Bobby in his hand and gently patted him. The bulb was barely hot. That didn't make sense. They had been shining for hours. Normally, Remington couldn't even touch them, let alone pick one up and put it in his hand. But, he was too tired to worry about it, so he patted the blue bulb one more time.

"I know you have listened to what I have told Old Bob. I know you know the truth. I hope you understand." Then, he used the back of his right hand to brush away the tears, and he returned to bed.

Bobby had still not told his family. This was the most difficult moment in his life. What he had to do was tougher than all the challenges he had faced while saving his family, his human friends, and even himself from the troubles and dangers they had experienced in the past.

Part of him couldn't believe what Remington was going to do to him and the entire Bright family. And yet, part of him also understood how Remington had come to his decision.

Maybe being in that office at the factory won't be so bad. He laughed. *And who knows, maybe they will have a hero's welcome for us when we return.*

At that moment he sensed a movement to his right and looked to see his mom stirring and turning to look at him. *"I am so tired. I wish Remington's mother would come turn off the lights so I could sleep. Aren't you tired? Why are you laughing?"*

"Yes, I am tired, but to tell you the truth, Mom, it's confusing. I was laughing, but there is nothing funny about what I have to tell you."

"I know I'm only half awake, and sleepy, but even so, what you said makes no sense. Maybe you can explain later. I'm going to try and get some sleep."

"No! No! I must tell you and all of our family right now. No matter how tired you are." He raised his voice and the words echoed through the tree branches. "All of you must listen to what I have to say. It is not good news."

It was one thirty in the morning. Remington's mom had trouble sleeping, and she had decided to come upstairs and turn off the Christmas tree lights. She walked into the room, and before checking on Remington, she reached to flick the switch on the wall and turn them off. But she hesitated when she looked closer at the bulbs. "My goodness! They almost look like they have run out of juice. They are barely lit."

She turned and walked to the side of the bed and looked down at her son. She pulled the covers up around his shoulders, and as she started to walk away, she noticed his cheeks. She bent over and looked closer. She ran the tips of her fingers over the left side of his face.

"It looks like you have been crying, my sweet little boy," she whispered. *I wonder if I should wake him up. Maybe he had a bad dream.*

She stood and looked at him for a few seconds. Then she whispered again, "Oh, I guess not." She turned and walked to the wall and turned off the lights.

Well before Remington's mom had walked into the room, every bulb, including tough old Uncle Flicker and ornery little Geeminy, had shed tears. It was no wonder that when she had looked at the bulbs they appeared to be covered with a light fog. There was no brilliance left in what had once been the world's brightest Christmas tree light bulbs.

"Go to sleep," yelled Bobby. Then he realized how silly it was to have shouted those words. Most of the bulbs were sleeping within moments after the switch had been turned off. A long, long day and the worst news of their lives had made it easy to fall asleep.

Bobby was alone with his thoughts. He really did understand where the little redhead was coming from. Remington was getting older. He was a good kid. Bobby had been impressed with him and liked him from the first moment he saw him. He could still picture him rushing in to the room with that red hair standing up straight on the top of his head and squealing with joy that he had a Christmas tree.

Boy, it was hard to believe that had been three years ago. This had been their fourth Christmas together.

"What a time we have had in this house," he said quietly, and he remembered the first nine years stuck at the back of the tree. Then he remembered escaping his pod and helping to save his family and ending up on Remington's tree. Then he remembered the greatest Christmas ever, and he remembered the year of heroics when all of the bulbs had saved Mrs. McGillicuddy, and he had saved his dad, cousin Whitening, and Remington. Then he remembered Spain and the scary night he saved Remington when he was lost in downtown Madrid, and the marvelous trips to bullfights, palaces, and huge parades. And then, he remembered being a professor and helping Remington say some words in Bulbese, and he remembered trying to squeak out some words in human language.

"*Oh, the memories.*" And then Bobby Bright dozed off into a deep sleep.

Epilogue

Remington partially opened his eyes. He could feel the tears on his cheeks. He wondered if he had fallen asleep crying after he had told Bobby that he wanted Old Bob to take the strand back to the town where they had been born.

He reached up and wiped a wet spot on his face. Then, he stretched his legs beneath the bed covers and pulled his arms outside the top blanket. He could see sunlight sneaking between the slats of the wooden blinds at the front of the bedroom.

He lay there for a few minutes just staring into space. He wasn't ready to get out of bed yet. Suddenly, he realized there was something wrong. He rolled off his stomach and turned over on his right side. It was then he noticed there was a strange blanket laying over him. It sure wasn't the blanket on his bed last night. In fact, he didn't ever remember seeing this blanket. He pushed up on his elbows and opened his eyes wide. He looked around the room. Now he knew something was definitely wrong. He closed his eyes for a moment.

When he opened them again, he could see the outline of his dad's basketball trophies from his high school days. "What are those doing there?" he mumbled to himself.

He closed his eyes once more and rolled all the way to his left side. His back was now to the window where the trophies sat. It was then his arm fell off the side of the bed and his right hand touched the floor. Something was wrong. This wasn't the big bed in the upstairs bedroom. This wasn't the bed that he had slept in for the past three years when coming to see his grandparents for Christmas.

He pushed the covers away and sat up straight. Where was the tree? Why was he in this small twin-size bed?

"What's going on? What's happening?" he mumbled to himself. Then he looked to be sure and knew for certain he wasn't wrong. There was no Christmas tree in the room. His eyes turned back to the window box covered with trophies. Why was he in his dad's old bedroom?

"Mom, Dad? What's going on?" he hollered.

In a matter of seconds he heard footsteps coming through the hall. The bedroom door opened and he saw his mom.

"What's wrong? Did you call me? I was just coming to get you out of bed for breakfast."

Before he could answer, his dad stepped through the doorway and peeked over his mom's shoulder. "Is there something wrong? Did you just yell for us? And why are you staring at us with that strange look on your face?"

"Where's my little Christmas tree? Where are Bobby and the bulbs? Why is this old bed in here? Where is the new, big, wide bed that Grandma and Grandpa bought? You know, Mom, the one you and Dad sleep in now. Why am I in this bed and not upstairs?"

His mom reached down and placed her hand on his forehead. "What are you talking about? Do you feel okay? Come on, it's time for breakfast."

"Is there something wrong in here?" Mrs. McGillicuddy came rushing into the bedroom, buttoning her robe and tugging at some curlers in her hair. "Did I hear Remington calling?"

Before anyone could answer, Mr. McGillicuddy hurried in behind her. "Is Remington all right? What's all the yelling about?"

"Grandpa, Grandma. I'm glad you're here. Where's Bobby?"

Remington's eyes darted from face-to-face, but nobody answered. His grandparents and parents exchanged glances with each other. There were weird expressions on every face in the room.

Finally, Mr. McGillicuddy spoke. "Hey, little buddy, who is Bobby?"

"What do you mean, Grandpa? Bobby, my magical blue bulb. He's my best friend."

Mr. McGillicuddy stood at the foot of the bed with a strange expression on his face. Remington pointed a finger at his grandfather and looked at him like he was crazy. "I mean, he's your friend too. You believe in Bobby more than Grandma or Mom or Dad."

"Lisa, what is he talking about?" Mrs. McGillicuddy turned to her daughter-in-law with a worried look on her face.

Before his mom could answer, Remington looked up to the ceiling and yelled, "Bobby, are you upstairs? I'm coming to see you. I'm coming up the stairs, right now. I've changed my mind. You don't have to go with Old Bob."

He pushed the bedcovers back, but his dad put his right hand on one of his shoulders and held Remington down. He felt Remington's forehead.

"Well, you don't have a fever," he said with a chuckle. "So, what are you talking about?"

Remington looked at his father but didn't answer. He pulled loose from him and quickly slid out of the bed. When his feet hit the floor, he looked down at them and shrieked, "Oh, my gosh! What's wrong with me? Why am I so short?"

He turned around and looked at his dad, and then he looked at his mom. He felt tears starting to well up in his eyes. He took two steps and bumped in to his grandfather but pulled away from him and raced around the foot of the bed and jumped into his dad's arms. He hugged him. Then he leaned back, and with one hand brushed away the tears. He started to ask another question but his dad interrupted.

"What's wrong? Just calm down and tell all of us what's going on."

"Something's really wrong here. I'm shorter than I'm supposed to be. I have a tree in the bedroom upstairs. I have a buddy named Bobby. You know all this. I'm almost eleven years old, and you've believed me about Bobby since I was seven. We all agreed last year when we lived in Spain that he is our family's miracle bulb. Ask Grandma, ask Grandpa."

"In Spain? What are you talking about? We've never lived in Spain." He reached to touch Remington's head again.

"Don't touch my head. I'm fine. I don't have a fever. Just tell me is this a joke or something?"

As he looked into his dad's eyes and waited for an answer he heard his mom start laughing. Remington looked across the room at her standing in front of the window box. "Why are you laughing at me?"

"I'm not really laughing at you, sweetheart," she said as she crossed the room and walked past the bed's footboard. She took Remington's hand. "Sit down between Daddy and me."

Remington looked into her eyes for a brief moment and nodded his head. He slipped out of his dad's arms, dropped to the floor, and sat back on the edge of the bed. He snuggled in between the two of them. His grand-parents stood in the bathroom doorway only a few feet away.

"Remington," his mom said, "first of all, you are only seven years old. We arrived here at Grandma and Grand-pa's late last night. You fell asleep in your grandpa's arms before we got you to bed." She took hold of both of his arms and pulled him close to her. "He brought you in here and put you in the same bed you sleep in every year when we come here for Christmas. But, I'm pretty sure I know what's happened."

Before she could say anything else, Remington pulled loose from her and again slid out of bed. He walked to the bathroom door where his grandfather was standing. He turned and looked back at his parents.

"Where's Maria and Old Bob? I gave Bobby and the bulbs to him, but I changed my mind. Grandma and Grandpa, you both know Grandma would have died if Bobby and the bulbs hadn't saved her after the tornado."

"Oh, my baby." His mom held her hands out. "Come on back over here to me."

He wiped some more tears from his face with the back of his right hand and then he slowly walked back to the bed. She patted him on his back and held him tightly in her arms.

"Shh!" she crooned. "Look in my eyes and listen to me, Remington McGillicuddy."

After blinking back some more tears, he did as she asked.

"I think I know what's happened."

"What? What? Tell me and let me go see my buddy Bobby and all the bulbs."

"I'm sorry. But there are no bulbs. I don't know who all those people are you're talking about. But I do know this. You have been dreaming."

"No! No! No! Mom. Listen to me. All of you, listen! It's not true."

But it was...

Or was it?

The End of the Bobby Bright Series

*A*uthor's Note to all my wonderful Bobby Bright readers:

Dreams can be so wonderful. Sure, they can sometimes be scary, but when you think of the happy and pleasant dreams you have had, you can have some wonderful memories.

Remington will live every day of his life always knowing he had a magical friend that helped him learn many things, even if they were in dreams.

Of course, you might also wish to think that Remington's mom was wrong. Maybe it wasn't a dream. That's why only you can decide: Was it or wasn't it?

SPECIAL WORDS AND PHRASES IN "BULBESE"

"Bulbese" is a very special language and it is impossible to translate more than a few words or phrases into human language.

Bobby Bright has been able to assist author John Brooks as he tries to learn a few words.

Following are the only known "Bulbese" words or sounds that can be understood by humans. Mr. Brooks and Remington McGillicuddy are the only humans who can understand the following sounds.

The "Bulbese" phrases and sentences are printed in dark letters. The pronunciation is in parentheses ( ). See the pronunciation key to say each word correctly. The meaning of each entry follows its pronunciation.

Beep'—de——beep'—-Beep
(bēp' di bēp' bēp >)
MERRY CHRISTMAS!

Beep'—-uhh—-de'——beep
(bēp' ə di' bēp)
WHAT IS YOUR NAME?

B-e-e-p/beep' de
(bē > pbep' di)
MY NAME IS ... .

Beep. ... Beep. ... Beep/Beep?'
(bēp > bēp > bēpbēp'?)
HOW OLD ARE YOU?

B-e-e-e-e-e-e-p ... ... Bee. ... Beep
(bē > ē > p > bē > bēp)
ARE YOU HAPPY?

B-e-e-e-p (pause) B-e-e-e-p (pause) Beep—de—-Beep?'
(bē > p % bē > p % bē > pdibēp?)
WHAT TIME IS IT?

B-e-e-e-p (pause) B-e-e-e-p (pause) B-e-e-e-e-e-p (pause)
B-e-e-e-e-e-e-p beep/beep'?
(bē > p % bē > p % bē > ē > p % bē > ē > ē > p bēpbēp'?)
DO YOU LIKE SCHOOL?

Beep B-e-e-e-e-e-e-e-e-e-e-e-e-p B-e-e-e-p
(bēp bē > ē > ē > ē > p bē > p)
I LOVE YOU.

B-e-e-e-p de' b-e-e-e-p de' beep/beep
(bē > p di' bē > p di' bēpbēp)
HAPPY BIRTHDAY!

Beep/Beep B-e-e-e-e-p
(bēpbēp bē > ē > p)
LET'S PLAY A GAME.

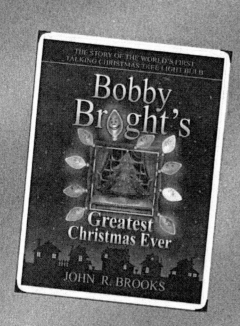

Our Family Picture

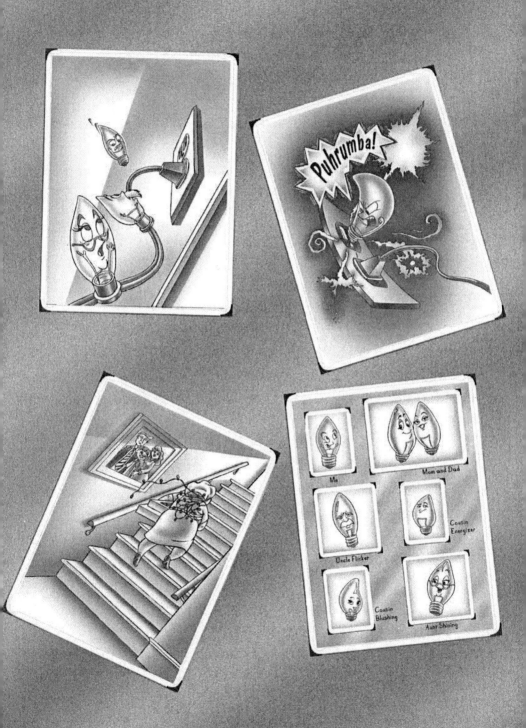

Carolyn,

*Read First
Then Flip It* 4

BOBBY BRIGHT
BECOMES A PROFESSOR
AND IS LOST AT SEA

BY
John R. Brooks

2017

ILLUSTRATIONS BY
Dan Daly, Troy Gustafson
and Jeff Elliott

Old Farm Press

Published by Old Farm Press
P.O. Box 20894| Oklahoma City, Oklahoma 73156 USA
1.405.748.7072 | www.bobbybrightbooks.com

Cover and interior design by Chris Webb
Illustrations by Jeff Elliott

Published in the United States of America

ISBN: 978-1-61346-753-4
1. Juvenile Fiction / Fantasy & Magic
2. Juvenile Fiction / Holidays & Celebrations / Christmas & Advent
16.11.11

Contents

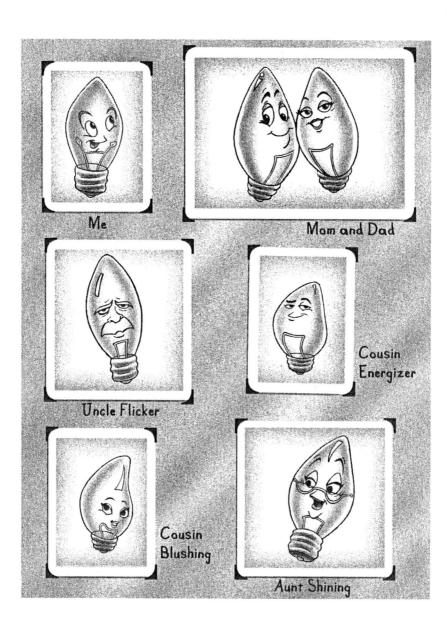

Prologue

Three Weeks Earlier

It was six thirty on the morning of January seventh.
"I'm so tired, Mom."

"Well, I told you. I tried to get you to go to bed at nine o'clock last night because you had to get up early."

"I know," said Remington as he took the final bite from what had once been three scrambled eggs on the plate in front of him. "It's just that I wanted to stay up and play those games with Grandpa and Grandma. I am going to miss them so much."

"We will miss you even more, Remington," said Mrs. McGillicuddy.

Remington turned his head, and in the doorway were both of his grandparents. "How long have you been standing there?"

"Since you were about halfway through those eggs," answered Mr. McGillicuddy, "And the way you were eating them, that's only been about half a minute."

Remington laughed. "I know, Grandpa, I love scrambled eggs." Then, he quickly shoved the chair back from the table and ran to the doorway and hugged his grandparents.

1

"Get up here in my arms, you big nine-year-old. I've got to lift you before you get much heavier," said Mr. McGillicuddy.

"So, Lisa," Mrs. McGillicuddy asked, "you and Richard are taking Remington to school and then coming back to take us to the airport?"

"No, we are all going together to school, and then we will go on to the airport. That way you get a few more minutes with Remington."

"Yeah! I'm glad, because I am going to miss you so much."

"Just promise us you will be a good boy, and you must take care of our miracle bulbs. Don't let them do anything crazy. In fact, since all of us believe they are a little mysterious, do you think maybe we should just take them with us to make sure they are safe?"

"No, Grandpa," Remington quickly answered. "You don't mean it, do you?"

A big grin broke out on Mr. McGillicuddy's face. "Just kidding, good buddy."

"Good, because when you come back this summer, you'll be able to hear Bobby say my name because I am going to teach him."

Mr. and Mrs. McGillicuddy started laughing, but Remington's mom had a frown on her face. "Oh, Remington! You are not going to make me believe a bulb can talk."

"Mom, I know he said 'Bobby' at least three times."

"No, you think you heard a noise, and you made yourself believe it sounded like the word *Bobby*."

"Oh, don't be too sure, Lisa," Mr. McGillicuddy interrupted. He paused and raised his eyebrows.

"When you raise your eyebrows like that, John McGillicuddy," his wife said, "you are being mischievous. What are you talking about?"

"Remington is going to have so much time to spend with those bulbs that I've got an idea."

"Remington," he said, peering down at his grandson, who was now standing near the kitchen table, "if you are going to teach Bobby some new words, then why don't you learn something new too, and have him teach you some words in his language?"

"Dad," Lisa said to her father-in-law, "you are making this even more difficult. Quit putting those thoughts in his mind."

"But, Mom, that's a great idea. I never thought of that, Grandpa. Maybe Bobby and the bulbs do have their own language."

"I can't believe I'm hearing this," said Remington's mother.

"Well, that makes two of us," said Mrs. McGillicuddy.

"Not me," added Mr. McGillicuddy. "I think I've had another great idea."

"Me too," said Remington, and then he started giggling. "What do you think they speak, Grandpa?"

Mr. McGillicuddy had a big smile on his face, and he winked at Remington with his right eye; and out of the corner of his other eye he saw his daughter-in-law and wife looking at him.

"You know, I wouldn't be surprised if those bulbs speak *Bulbese.*"

Our Family Picture

1

A New Place to Study

The second morning after his grandparents returned to America, Remington heard the noise for the first time. Loud voices awakened him about 7:30 at least half an hour before he normally got out of bed to get ready for school.

He listened but was unable to understand any of the words being spoken, but he could certainly hear the noise. It was loud. Truck doors were being opened and closed. Lots of workmen were chattering away in Spanish. And by the second day, the noise got louder as the sound of power saws cutting wood drowned out the voices of the workers.

There was no chance to go back to sleep once the noise started, and when he got out of bed he could see lots of men down on the sidewalk. They were dragging ladders and other equipment into the building directly across the street.

He saw two small trucks parked on the sidewalk. Two of their wheels were just barely off the curb. It was the only way other cars could pass down the narrow one-lane

street that ran in front of the four-story apartment building.

Suddenly, the door opened behind him, and he heard his mom's voice.

"I wondered if that noise would wake you early."

"Just like it did yesterday, Mom. What's going on?

She joined him by the window, and together they stepped out on to the tiny balcony that overlooked *Fomento*. "I didn't really get a chance to tell you yesterday, but I had heard a few weeks ago that a new café and *tapas* bar was going to be built. I guess this proves the rumor true."

"You mean we are going to have a restaurant right across the street?"

"Not really a restaurant. Oh, they will serve food because there will be lots of *tapas*, but probably that's it. Not a big menu. Mostly a place for people in the neighborhood to go for snacks and drinks."

"How long will it take to fix that building up?"

"I have no idea. You know how these Spaniards are. They are going to work early, maybe take a *siesta* in the afternoon, and probably work until after eight in the evening."

Remington started to say something, but his mom continued, "You might as well go ahead and get ready for school. You are going to be waking up earlier than normal until they finish."

"But, Mom. What if it's going to be like this every afternoon? I couldn't concentrate when I tried to study yesterday. If it's this noisy I can't study in here."

"Well, I've been thinking about that, and I have an idea. How would you like to start doing your homework in the ballroom?"

"Are you serious? You'd let me up there?"

"Well, your dad and I have been thinking about putting a desk in there so Maria could use it. It could even be like a classroom for the two of you while she teaches you Spanish."

"Hey, that is a good idea."

"Well, we'll see. Right now, you've got to get ready for school."

2

A Longer Time in Spain

Remington's mother walked to the landing between the second and third floors of the apartment. She yelled up the staircase, "Remington, come downstairs. I forgot to tell you something."

As she started walking back down the staircase, she heard the scrape of a chair in the ballroom upstairs and then the feet of Remington as he hurried through the room and came bouncing down the steps.

"Were you doing your homework?" she asked as he joined her in the living room.

"Yeah, Mom. Maria had already finished my Spanish lesson, and I was working on the rest of my homework. I love working upstairs in that old ballroom. It is quiet, and I don't have to listen to the noise from the street. Do you think they will ever finish?"

"Well, of course they will finish. But it's only been three weeks since they started. I watched from your bedroom window today, and they are doing a lot of work; but it's going to take them some time before the café is completed.

"But listen to me. I called you down here to make sure you get your homework finished quickly. I forgot to tell you that Daddy wants to take us to dinner tonight after he gets home from the embassy. He is working until eight o'clock.

"That means there will be no chance for you to do anything but go to bed after we get back from dinner. So, get back up there and make sure all your work is done so you will be ready."

"Yippee! Can we go eat at *Topolinos?* I like all the different things on that buffet."

"Well, I'm not sure. Your daddy said he had some real good news and that maybe we would go to *El Botin.*"

"Really? That would be awesome. It's so neat eating in that cave downstairs. Mom, is it really the oldest restaurant in the world? I mean, I know they say so, but really?"

"I guess, Remington. Everyone in Spain claims it's true, and there are books and sites on the Internet that verify it."

"How old, Mom?"

"Well, you can figure that up yourself. It opened in 1725. I always remember the date because—"

But Remington interrupted her before she could finish the sentence. "Because that is the address of our house in America."

"That's the exact reason. Now I didn't call you down-stairs just to tell you about going out to eat tonight." She got up from the couch and walked toward the kitchen. "Follow me, I have some other good news."

She reached into her purse, which was sitting on the kitchen counter, and waited for Remington to come through the doorway. Then she handed Remington an envelope.

"It's a letter from Grandpa and Grandma. Do you see who it is addressed to?"

"Oh, wow! It's addressed to me."

"So, open it. Let's find out what's happening in America."

"Daddy, you're home." Remington rushed down the stairs and jumped into his dad's arms.

"Hey, have you been eating too much? You are getting heavier. We may have to put you on a diet before your birthday."

"Dad, I'm not heavy. I'm still the skinniest kid in my class at school."

"I know, just kidding. But you are getting heavier. At least Spain has put a few pounds on you."

"I think it may be those pastries that Mom and I have been eating every day since Maria came to live with us."

"*Es verdad, señor.* I fix the best *tortas.*"

"Maria," Remington's mom said as their nanny walked in from the kitchen, "you and Remington don't need to be telling Daddy secrets."

His parents kissed, and Remington asked, "Are we really going to *El Botin* for dinner?"

"Yes, I have some news. I think it is good, although I have mixed feelings."

"What is it?"

"No, dear, I'm keeping quiet until we get to the restaurant. Then I will tell you." Before either his wife or only son could say anything, Richard McGillicuddy smiled and said, "So, let's get going. After dinner, Remington, I am going to buy you one of those giant, creamy tarts that you like so much from our favorite bakery in *Plaza Mayor.*"

"He like the tart more than me?" Maria asked.

"No, Maria," Remington said with a chuckle. "I like you more than the tart."

"No, no, no. I mean you like that creamy tart more than my *tortas?*"

"No, but they are good."

"I don't know if good. That restaurant and those *pastelerias* are for rich people."

"We are not rich, Maria, but you are getting a chance to eat that tart and some fabulous food tonight because you are going with us."

"You mean it, Mom? Maria is going to *El Botin?*"

"Your mom is right," answered his dad. "We are all going."

"Oh, *señor*, you no do it. *Es demasiado caro.*"

"Maria, you are going with us, and it is not too expensive.

"You know, Daddy, maybe I could get two *tortas*. My birthday is only three weeks away."

His parents laughed.

"You've started the countdown," his mom said.

"Yep. It's getting closer to double-digit time."

"Double digits. I can't believe it," she said. "Remember last year when we tried to explain double digits to you?"

"Yes. I must have been a dummy not to know it meant when you reach ten years old."

"Okay, my soon-to-be-ten-year-old son," said his dad, "let's go to the cave." He opened the closet door in the living room and grabbed the coats for his wife and Remington.

"I will get my *abrigo*, uh ... coat, *señor*. Wait a minute, please." Maria hurried upstairs to her room to get her only winter coat out of the closet. The entire way she kept thinking about the conversation moments earlier. *How will I ever understand all these English sayings? What is 'double digit'?*

"*Todo esta bien, Señor?*"

"*Si, claro,*" Remington's dad answered, and one of the many waiters with their long aprons covered with stains of *pollo* and *cuchillo* nodded his head and walked away from the table.

The four of them were seated at the very rear of one of the rooms in the cave below the first floor of the world's oldest restaurant. On the table were four of the *tapas* listed on the menu. Remington's dad had insisted that each person order a favorite appetizer. The table was filled with tiny meatballs, *camarones*, or shrimp, mussels, and Remington's favorite, *calamari*.

"Now that the appetizers are here, do we have to eat everything before you tell us the big news?"

"Okay, dear, I'm ready. But I have to tell you there is good and bad news."

"Tell us the good news first, Daddy."

"What do you think, Lisa?"

"Yeah, Mom, what do you think? Good or bad news first?"

Before she could answer, Remington said, "Excuse me, Mom, but Daddy, would you pass me some more *calamari?*"

"Don't eat too much and spoil your appetite. You've got half of a roast chicken to eat."

"Don't worry, Mom, I love the squid, and I am starving. I'll still be able to eat the *pollo.*"

"All right, now can I continue with my news?"

"Okay, Dad. You make the choice, good or bad."

"Well, thank you," and the three of them laughed.

Maria smiled, but she appeared to not quite understand everything. Remington's dad noticed and said, "I'll explain later, Maria, if you have trouble understanding."

Remington interrupted one more time. "I've changed my mind. Start with the bad news first."

"Sorry, buddy, but I think I had better reverse it. The good news is we now know when I will be finished here in Madrid and when we will be returning to America."

He paused and waited for a reaction, but no one said anything. Everyone just looked at him.

"Why are you staring at me? Did you hear what I said?"

"Yes, dear, except we have been planning to go home after Remington gets out of school in late June."

"Well," and he cleared his throat, wiped some crumbs from the fried *calamari* that was hanging on his lip, and continued. "You see, that is the bad news."

"What?"

"What are you saying, Dad?"

"I'm saying that we won't be going back home until just before Christmas."

"What?" Lisa snapped. "But I told everyone we would be home by the start of school next fall."

"Oh, boy," Remington interrupted. "Will Grandpa and Grandma ever be angry if we don't come to their house for Christmas. I told them I would make sure to bring

Bobby and all the bulbs back so they can be on my very own tree."

"Oh, Remington, please. Don't start talking about those bulbs right now. Richard, what happened?"

"The ambassador wants me to remain at the embassy and clear up some loose ends when our project is over in the fall. But don't panic. I'm ninety-nine percent sure we will be leaving by the end of November, so we will be home for Christmas. It just may be a little hectic."

"Good. That's not so bad after all. It means I will have more time to experience this culture."

Remington's dad started laughing.

"What is so funny, Daddy?"

"Yes, what is so funny, Richard? This changes all of our plans. What is funny about that?"

"Oh, it's just Remington. I liked your 'experience this culture' statement. I just thought it sounded very grown up. It's true. We will have more time to enjoy Madrid and see some other parts of Spain. Plus, there is nothing I can do about it."

"Look, Mom, here comes the food."

"Good. We can talk about this later."

As two waiters approached with plates of roast-suckling pig, rotisserie chicken, and vegetables, and placed them on the table, Remington's dad promised, "Everything will be fine. We'll be home before Christmas. Now do you feel better?"

"A little better," said his mom.

Everyone but Maria started eating. She just sat there. She had not even picked up her fork, let alone taken a bite of food.

"Maria, what is wrong?"

Her head was tilted down, and she was staring at her plate. Remington's mom repeated the question. "What is wrong?"

Remington saw his nanny reach for the napkin in her lap, and she quickly wiped her face and the corner of her eyes.

"What's wrong, Maria? Are you crying?"

"Uh…no, I be fine. I say prayer."

"Oh, Maria, how sweet. You blessed our food?"

"No, *señora*, not the food."

"What's wrong, Maria? Was it really a prayer, or are you crying?

"It is both, *señor. ¿Permiteme decirle en español?*"

"Go ahead, I will tell them in English."

"*Yo digo un orácion para los dias pasan lentimiento. Les echare de menos a Ustedes. Nunca sera lo mismo la vida despues al fin de Noviembre. Lo siento para mis lágrimas.*"

"No, *te preocúpes. Hay posibilidades que incluso tumismo en nuestros planos.*"

"Oh, *señor, lo dudo mucho.*"

"Richard, please! Tell us what is wrong. What is she saying?"

"Maria was praying for the days to go slowly."

It took a moment, but then Remington's mom exclaimed, "Oh, my goodness! She is worried we will leave her in November, isn't she?"

"I think so."

"Yes, *señora*. That I worry."

"She said she will miss us, and her life will never be the same. She even apologized for the tears."

"I have an idea," Remington broke into the conversation. "Why don't you move to the United States with us, Maria?"

"Oh, it not possible *mi pelirrojo*."

"Remington, you're a smart young man," his dad smiled at him and then looked back at their nanny. "Maria, Mrs. McGillicuddy and I have been talking about that very thing. It could happen."

"No, *me digas, señor. Es un milagro, si se realiza*."

"Well, miracles are known to happen, and I think this one will."

Suddenly, throughout the underground cave that was the basement of the world's oldest restaurant, other diners looked on in amazement. They saw a man, a woman, and a young child standing and looking at the tiny old woman sitting at their table. The three of them applauded her as she wiped away the tears pouring down her weathered and pockmarked face, which had suffered so much in recent years.

"Are you sure we will be home for Christmas? I told all of our friends we would be back, and I know your folks won't come because they are coming back in June."

"Look, honey, I'm sure everything will be fine. It's only February. It's not like Christmas is next month. Now, please let me go to sleep."

Remington heard his dad and mom talking as he tip-toed past his parents' bedroom door. He had been in bed for more than half an hour and still couldn't fall asleep. All he could think about was the creamy vanilla tart he had brought home from the restaurant. He had been too full to eat it after dinner. He sneaked down the stairs and into the first-floor living room.

Off to his left, he caught sight of light underneath the kitchen door. When he opened the door, he knew why the light was on. There, at the table, sat Maria. She was crying.

"Maria, what is wrong?"

She turned her head and looked at him, and with the back of her hand, wiped away the tears on her right cheek. She smiled. "*No te preocupes.*"

"What do you mean? I'm not worried. I just want to know what is wrong. I thought you were through crying. *¿Que es el problema?*"

"There is no problem. I just sad, you see. You, and your parents leaving Madrid."

"But that is not until just before Christmas. That is over eight months away. Plus, you heard Daddy. He means what he says. I know he does. You will come to my country."

"*Yo lo se.*"

"Well, if you know," Remington continued, "then why cry now?"

"The time, it veel move fast than think you."

"Maria," Remington corrected, "the time will move faster than you think."

"That is what I say, Remington."

He started giggling.

"What you geeggle for?"

Remington remembered teaching Maria the word *giggle*, and she loved to use it.

"What? What you geeggle for?"

Remington had his head tucked down and was still giggling. "You make me laugh when I correct you sometimes."

She wiped another tear away from her other cheek and looked straight at Remington. Then she laughed. "I don't understand why, but I know this: *te amo mucho.*"

"I love you too. Don't worry anymore about it. You thought we were moving back to America in June. Now it will be longer, and you can still enjoy your country until November and then move to my country."

"Oh, I hope so, *mi pelirrojo*."

As they walked together to the kitchen door, she reached to turn off the light, and then she suddenly stopped. "*¿Porque vengas aqui?*"

"I came here because I couldn't sleep. I started getting hungry."

"I know. You came for the..."

"For the *torta*. It's still in the refrigerator, isn't it?"

"No. It is gone."

"What? Did you eat it?"

Then she smiled and said, "See, I geet just like you. I like to keed you like you keed me."

"Say *get*, not *geet*; and *kid*, not *keed*, okay?" Before she could react to his corrections, he said, "But it's true. You got me this time. I will share it with you, and then you can take me to my room and tuck me in to bed."

"I tuck you in bed. It is funny American word. But I tuck you in bed."

3
Why Won't He Talk?

It was February seventh.

"I don't understand why you don't say anything." Remington held the blue Christmas tree light bulb close to his face.

Moments earlier, he had turned off the lights and let them cool for a moment before he had unscrewed Bobby. They had been shining just as brightly tonight as they had for a month since Remington's grandparents had returned to the United States.

He rolled the blue bulb around in the palm of his right hand. Then he tossed it a few inches in the air and caught it. He held it between two fingers and stared at it. "I have to go downstairs and eat. Please," he pleaded, "when I get back from supper, try and at least say *Bobby* to me."

Then, he held the bulb close to his mouth and said, "Just please say something, anything. You're here with me because Grandpa and Grandma thought I would love having you with me, even when it isn't Christmas time.

You know, I have finally made all of my family believe you really are 'miracle' bulbs. Even my mom almost believes you've said your name in human language."

Remington laughed quietly and held the bulb back out in front of him. "Well, maybe only a little bit, but Grandpa definitely believes me. So, here we are, together every day, and after a month, you still haven't said your name. I want to hear you say it, and then maybe I could teach you some other words too. It's perfect, and we've got four more months until summer when my grandparents come back to visit. But when they leave, they will be taking you back home to the United States so they can put you on my tree at Christmas.

"So, come on, please," pleaded Remington. "All of you bulbs get to shine every night, and you are not locked away in a dark, old closet. So, you owe me a big favor." Remington once again put the bulb close to his face and whispered, "Don't you want to say at least a couple of different words?"

Just then he heard Maria's voice outside the bedroom door. He ran to the window and quickly started screwing the bulb back into the empty socket.

"Remington. Remington. *Venga!* It is time the supper to eat, now."

Remington laughed. He loved hearing Maria speak English. She was getting better, but she still placed words in the wrong part of sentences.

"I'm coming," he shouted and opened the door. She was standing there, smiling, with an apron covering most of her long dress, which nearly touched the tops of her shoes.

"There you be, *pelirrojo*.

"Maria, why do you always call me *pelirrojo?*"

"I tell you before this."

Remington interrupted her before she could continue. "No, Maria, you say, 'I have told you this before.' That is the correct way."

"*Bueno.* I have told you this before," she said very slowly and pronounced each word perfectly.

"Very good."

"Thank you," she said. "Now, you want the reason to know, or no?"

Remington chuckled. "Go ahead, tell me again."

"The first time I see you—"

Remington interrupted her once more. "The first time I saw you.' *Saw*, not *see*; do you understand?"

"Thank you, yes. The first time I saw you in that street all alone. I see you crying, but even before, you know what I see first?"

"That I was a redhead, right?"

"*Es correcto mi cariño.*"

"Yes, I am correct."

"And you are a dear boy. Now, come you with me. *Tiene hambre?*"

"Yes, I am hungry."

Bobby looked at his mom in the next pod.

"You know, I can't keep doing this."

She twisted to her left and looked at him. "What do you mean?"

"You know what I mean. You tell me I can't speak to him. He wants to teach me other words in his language. Why can't I try?"

Bobby's dad tried to lean forward and look around his mother. It was still hard to do, even after two years since part of his head had been smashed. But he managed and he said, "I agree with Bobby."

Bobby smiled. "Well, thank you."

"In fact, I think it is time to see if this boy, Remington, is as smart as you. Go ahead and speak to him. Say your name."

"Are you serious?"

"Yes, dear, are you serious?" his mom asked.

"Well, I think you should tell him my name."

"See what you have started, Dad. Now Twinkle wants to be involved. I'll just say to him, 'Let me introduce you to one of my sisters. See, there she is right next to my dad.'"

"Thank you, brother. I'm sure he would like to know my name, too. That's perfect."

"Get real."

"Well don't forget your wonderful brother. Introduce me too."

"Oh, now I have a family of funny bulbs," Bobby said, laughing.

"How about me?"

"Oh, I won't forget you, Sparkle. My first words to Remington will be, 'Meet my two sisters and my dear brother, Dimmer."

"You be careful." The tone of his mom's voice made Bobby shift in his pod. "I still think we would be in trouble if Remington's parents really believed you could talk."

"Well, if that's the case, we are all in trouble. What if they knew we spoke Bulbese?"

"You know what I mean. No human can understand Bulbese, and no human is going to believe we can speak our own language."

Bobby turned and looked at his mother again. "You know, it really doesn't matter. How in the world could I tell Remington anything in human language, anyway? I got lucky one time and squeaked my name to him nearly three years ago. Maybe I've been able to do it a couple of times since. So, I know it would be difficult for him to understand me, although I admit it would be fun to learn and say at least one other word."

"Well, despite the fact Mr. McGillicuddy is supposedly on our side and believes you have magical powers…"

Bobby interrupted her. "No. He believes we all have magical powers."

"Whatever. I'm not sure that just because he may think we are different that it makes it right for you to start beeping words in Bulbese and make it sound like human language."

"Why not? You know Remington, he will probably not say anything to his parents, anyway."

"Oh, really? Remington has told his parents and grand-parents you spoke your name to him ever since the first time we were on his little Christmas tree. If you say another word, or words, he will definitely tell his parents. But to think you can learn anything else is ridiculous."

"Oh, you never know. Maybe I will become a professor and teach Remington Bulbese."

"Oh, that would be fun," chipped in Dimmer. "We'd have two professors in the same room. Wouldn't it be great if next Christmas he could say 'Merry Christmas' in Bulbese?"

"Hey! That's a super idea."

"You know what?"

"What?" He twisted and looked at Aunt Glaring in the pod to his left.

"I wondered why you hadn't given me your opinion."

"I was thinking and not talking. I've decided since Remington now has a nanny that she could teach you some Spanish too."

28

"Very funny. I think I better try saying my sisters' and brother's names first in English."

Dimmer spoke up again. "I still think you should teach him 'Merry Christmas' before any other words..."

"Do you agree? Are you listening to me?"

"Just mulling it over, but I agree with you. You're right. It makes sense. I mean we are Christmas tree light bulbs, and our most enjoyable time is being with Remington at Christmas."

"Listen, I am tired of leaning forward trying to talk to you. It's settled then, right?"

"Lean back, Dad. Relax. I guess you're right."

"Why you know I'm right, Bobby. We are having the best time we've ever had here in Spain. We get the chance to light up almost every day. We don't have to live in a dark closet like we did in the past. It's the best it has ever been. We will probably never again get to spend a year out of the closet. This will be your only chance to say some words. And, you might as well go for all of it. And take Dimmer's advice. Try to teach Remington some Bulbese."

As Bobby listened to his father, he was aware of something that had become more evident in recent days. Even though he still had trouble shifting or moving in his pod, his dad's voice was stronger, and he was speaking clearer. The accident he had suffered during the tornado nearly two years ago had left him speechless for

many weeks. Over time, he had gotten better, but Bobby wondered if being able to lie on Remington's windowsill and light up almost every day was the reason for the latest improvement.

His thoughts were interrupted when Uncle Flicker's booming voice bellowed from the opposite end of the plug.

"*Your dad is absolutely right. Go for it, my amazing and unbelievable nephew. You are the world's most intelligent Christmas tree light bulb. Prove it.*"

And the next evening, Bobby began to do just that.

4

Lesson Number One

February eighth would be a day to remember. Remington had gone straight to his room when he got home from school. He normally would unlock the front door and then go immediately to the kitchen so he could find something to eat like a *torta* or some other *pasteleria*.

However, today he had said "hello" to Maria and his mom as he raced through the living room and headed for his second floor bedroom. It was Maria who opened the kitchen door and shouted, "Where are you going?"

His mom's question followed. "Don't you want a snack?"

"Not now, I have to study." Then he was out of sight and into his room. He immediately went to the bulbs and plugged them in. Before they warmed up, he unscrewed Bobby from his pod. "Come with me, Bobby. I'm through messing around. Today, you are going to learn how to say 'Merry Christmas.' As for the rest of you bulbs, enjoy shining."

Suddenly Remington laid the blue bulb back on the windowsill. "Just a minute, I need to wash my hands."

Remington hurried to the bathroom and as soon as the water started running, Bobby whispered to his parents. *"He just said he was going to teach me how to say Merry Christmas."*

Bobby started to say something else but stopped when he heard the water turn off. A moment later, Remington returned and put the blue bulb in his pocket, grabbed a notebook and a pen, and hurried out of the room.

"Can you believe it?" Bobby's dad started laughing. *"You see, I was right yesterday. It's Bobby's time to learn some human language words."*

"Oh, you are brilliant, dear." Bobby's mom twisted in her pod and looked at her husband. *"Like father, like son. I bet Bobby will have some stories for us when he gets back tonight."*

Remington had been alone with Bobby in the huge ball-room for nearly an hour. He had raced downstairs and taken only a few seconds to tell Maria and his mom that he had a big homework project and needed to be left alone. Learning Spanish would have to wait until tomorrow.

His mom had asked what the project was, but he told her it was a surprise and that he would tell her later. Then Maria had smiled at him and gave him one of her *tortas* and some *leche* to take with him.

He was just now finishing the final bite out of the creamy tart, which had been filled with strawberries. He had been so busy trying to teach Bobby how to say "Merry Christmas" that when he swallowed the last drop of *leche,* it tasted warm and icky. "Ugh! I waited too long to finish the milk. I will be back in a moment," he said and headed out of the room, leaving the blue bulb lying on the desk.

Bobby watched Remington hurry out of the room holding the plate and glass in one hand and closing the door with his other hand. He waited to make sure he heard Remington going down the stairs.

"I know I can do this." He wasn't really sure he could, but he knew the time had come to try and quit wondering. *"Here goes,"* he said and took a deep breath and shouted, *"Puhrumba!"*

He waited for at least three seconds, but nothing happened. *This is strange,* he thought. *Puhrumba* was the word he always used when he needed to do something magical. For the briefest of moments, he thought he might be losing his special powers but quickly realized he was okay when he tried in a deeper and louder voice. *"Puhrumba!"* Almost immediately, he began to move, and he was able to quickly tilt up into a sitting position.

That's better, he thought. *"I still have my old powers. Now it's time to do it."* And before he could change his mind, or think anymore about it, he just up and said it.

"*Muuurrreee Keeetsmuuss!*" It took him a few seconds to realize what he had actually done, and he didn't know whether to laugh or be scared. "*I did it,*" he whispered in Bulbese and smiled. "*Oh, boy, did that ever sound strange.*"

It wasn't great, but at least it was a start, and within half a minute, his squeaky voice had repeated the words three more times.

It still didn't sound anything like the way Remington had said it, but Bobby hoped he was getting better. One thing for sure, he had his mind made up. He wanted to surprise Remington when he came back into the room.

"*Okay. One more time.*" He needed to hurry because he heard footsteps coming up the stairs. "*Muuurrreee Keetsmuuss!*"

He was pleased with how it sounded, but he sure wanted to try at least once again before Remington reached the hallway door. He took a deep breath, and just to give himself more confidence, he crossed his filaments and whispered, "*Muurree Kreestmuuss.*" He smiled as he saw the handle turn on the door. He let himself gently roll back onto his side, and he knew that was the best he had said it yet.

"I promise, Mom. I'm doing my homework," Remington shouted back to his mother and Maria as he again hurried through the dining room. He looked back and saw the door to the kitchen swing closed. He raced back up the stairs. "I know he can say it if he wants to," he muttered to himself as he rounded the second floor landing.

By the time he had reached the third floor, he was panting. He stopped outside the ballroom door to catch his breath, and it was then he heard the squeaking sound for the first time. At first, he wasn't sure what it was, but when he heard it again and listened closely, he was surprised.

"Oh, my gosh. That's Bobby," he whispered to himself. "I can't believe it. I can actually hear him. He's trying to say 'Merry Christmas' in English."

Remington started to giggle but stopped when he heard the voice again. There was no doubt this time. The same strange and squeaky sound he had heard over two years ago when he had heard the word *Bobby* was now the same voice squeaking, "Merry Christmas."

"I've done it. I can't believe it. I've taught him all by myself!"

Remington grinned and flung the door open. "I heard you, my best buddy. I just heard you. I've taught you how to say your first words other than your name. Oh, boy! Are we ever going to have fun!"

5
Hearing Things

Remington's dad unlocked the front door and had barely opened it before Remington came jumping into his arms.

"Whoa! What's all this about? Did I win a prize for best dad in Spain?"

"And America," Remington said, and laughed.

"Well, thank you."

"I just wanted to give you a hug. I'm upstairs studying with Maria, and she was thirsty for some *jugo de naranja*. So, I came down to get it, and you opened the door just as I was going into the kitchen."

"Well, I'm glad you timed it perfectly. I needed a hug. I had a tough day at the embassy. In fact, orange juice sounds really good. Why don't you pour me a glass too, before you take one to Maria?"

"Okay, Dad." Remington raced away to the kitchen just as his mom walked into the living room.

"Aren't you home early?"

"Yes, I couldn't seem to get anything done this after-noon. It's been a tough day, and I thought I would finish some work here at home tonight."

"I was lying down in the bedroom trying to take a nap and heard the door open. Then I heard Remington's voice."

"Anything wrong?"

"Yes, I'm hearing things," she quickly answered, and then smiled at her husband.

"That's it? That's your answer," he laughed. "Am I missing something here?"

"No, for the third straight day I have been hearing weird noises coming through the vent in the kitchen."

"The vent? You mean the one next to the stove?"

"Yes, the same one where we heard the voices of your mom and dad in their bedroom when they were here for Christmas. Remember Juan told us when we first moved in that there were air ducts from top to bottom in three places in the house, and you could hear noises sometimes from the floors above."

"Okay, but except for the folks at Christmas, had you heard any voices or noises until this week?"

"No, not until Maria and Remington started using the ballroom for a study area."

"Well, then what's strange about hearing Maria and Remington? You've heard them before."

"Except this wasn't Maria."

"Well, then you heard Remington talking to himself?" He laughed and put his arms around his wife. "Was he talking to himself?"

"No," she pulled loose and looked into his eyes. "Unless he has a squeaky voice that sounds like a mouse."

"What are you talking about?"

"I told you. I am hearing strange little noises. In fact, yesterday I went all the way upstairs to see what was going on, but Remington was in his room reading a book, and Maria was outside the front door mopping the hallway."

"So, what did you find in the ballroom? Mice?"

"Richard, don't make fun of me. It's strange."

"I'm sorry, dear."

"No one was there. Remington's books were on the desk, and that blue bulb, the amazing 'Bobby,' as Remington calls him, was lying next to one of the books."

"Oh, my gosh! Do you think it was Bobby who was talking?" He started to laugh some more but stopped when he saw tears come into her eyes. "Okay. Just kidding. I believe you. You heard noises."

"Well, I did."

"What noises, Mom?" Remington came through the kitchen doorway with two glasses of orange juice. "This one's for you, Dad."

"Thanks, Remington."

"I'm taking the other one to Maria," he said to his mom.

"Oh, is she back upstairs in the ballroom?"

"Yes. What noises are you talking about?"

"I have been hearing some squeaking sounds from upstairs the last three days."

Remington's mouth almost flew open, but he managed to keep it shut. He hoped he wasn't blushing, and he definitely kept from looking directly into his mother's eyes. "Oh," he said with his head tucked downward and his eyes focused on the glass of orange juice. "Well, I have to go and study." And he hurried out of the room.

"Be careful and don't spill that orange juice."

"Here, Maria." Remington walked into the ballroom and put the glass on the desk.

"*Gracias.*" Remington turned and blocked her view. He picked up Bobby and quickly walked toward the door.

"Come back here," Maria said. "You need to study."

"Be right back," he turned his head and yelled from the doorway. "I need to get one more book."

As soon as he closed the ballroom door, he whispered to Bobby. "Be careful up here when you are practicing. The sound goes down the air vent into the kitchen. My mom has been hearing you squeaking and trying to say human words."

At that moment, Maria opened the door. "I think you go get book."

"I remembered it was already up here," he answered and turned and walked past her and back into the ballroom.

6

A Nervous Bobby Bright

Bobby had never been more nervous. His mom tried to calm him down when they heard Remington's footsteps on the staircase.

"You will be fine. Just do this like you have done all the other marvelous things that you have accomplished."

"That's easy for you to say; you don't have to take the test."

"Well, I'm just trying to help."

"I'm sorry, I didn't mean to be rude. I'm just nervous."

Bobby's father joined in the conversation. *"Your mother's right. Just remember all the magical things you have done. You have been in dangerous spots before. This is not like saving Mrs. McGillicuddy. This sure isn't like using Rocket to help you get Mr. McGillicuddy in the house when you saved Remington at Christmas two years ago."*

"You're right." He leaned forward and looked at his dad. *"I know."* He started to say something else, but Aunt Glaring interrupted him.

"And it's certainly not like you having to fly into that wall socket on the most important day of all of our lives. I mean that was the day you saved us from being thrown away. How could you think this would be more difficult?"

"Wow, keep reminding me of all those things, and you are going to embarrass me."

"Robert...uhh...I mean, Bobby. No one is trying to embarrass you. We all know what you can do, so just go take your very first human language test and get it done."

Bobby smiled and thought to himself how much things had changed in the past year between he and his cousin, Dazzling. She had become a great friend instead of a troublesome relative. "Okay," he said, and leaned forward and grinned at her sitting in the middle of the strand. Then he shouted for all the bulbs to hear, "Dazzling is acting like a coach in one of those human sports. She just gave me a pep talk." He paused for a brief moment and then continued. "You know, it must have worked. I'm ready. I wish Remington would get here and give me my test."

Within seconds, the door opened, and Remington, with his red hair all ruffled up and needing to be combed, scampered into the bedroom and hurried to the window-sill where the strand was lying.

"I hope you are ready, Bobby." He unscrewed the bulb and was putting it in his pocket when his mom came into the room.

"Talking to those bulbs again?" she asked. "Are they answering you and telling you what they want to do today?"

"Go ahead, Mom. Make fun of me. You will just never understand."

She laughed again. "I love you, Remington McGillicuddy. It's okay, enjoy your bulbs, but do me a favor."

"What?" He turned around and looked across the room at her.

"You are going upstairs to start on your homework, aren't you?"

"Yes, but I don't have very much to do. I want to eat a *torta* first."

"That's fine, but I want you to get your other homework finished quickly because Maria is at the grocery store, and when she returns, she won't have a lot of time to teach you Spanish today."

"Why, what's wrong?"

"Nothing is wrong. It's just that she has a surprise for us tonight. For a long time she has wanted to cook us a special dinner. Tonight is the night, and she will need to be in the kitchen longer than normal. So, I want you to do your Spanish homework with her as soon as she gets back."

"Don't worry, Mom. I'm going up right now. I've got a lot to do upstairs today."

"I thought you said you didn't have much homework."

"Well, I don't, but then I do, I guess. I don't know. You are confusing me."

"Well, I will fix you a snack before you start your homework. Then, I'm going to take a quick nap while Maria prepares dinner. I didn't sleep well last night."

"Okay, Mom. I'll be right back down."

"Well, hurry, and while you're up there," she said as she watched Remington scamper up the stairs, "please comb your hair. It looks like it got caught in the food blender."

7

Bobby Takes His First Test

Bobby was lying on his side, nestled against one of Remington's history books. It was the waiting that was making things worse. Why couldn't Remington do his homework later? Why couldn't he give him his test right now? He was trying to practice his words as he whispered them, but it still wouldn't be the same as taking the test.

Just then, Remington reached down and picked up the blue bulb. "Don't worry, Bobby. I'm almost finished. Then it's going to be your turn. Your big moment is here. Just think of it. Over the past month, you have been able to say five different words or phrases in human language. Now I'm going to find out how well you have been listening to me because I have a little surprise in the test I'm giving you."

Remington started to say something else, but he heard the door handle turn. He quickly slid the bulb into his pocket as the door opened. "Hi, Maria. You're here earlier than I thought. I'm almost done with my other homework."

"No, te preocúpes cariño. I too busy with the surprise dinner. No Spanish lesson today. I go now."

Before Remington had time to say anything, she was back out the door and headed down the hallway. Remington got up and walked over to the door and shut it.

He pulled the blue bulb back out of his pocket and looked at it. "You're lucky, Bobby. That gives us more time for the test."

"So, did you pass the test?"

"Don't keep us in suspense. Did you pass or fail?"

"Tell us now. We want to know."

Questions in Bulbese were flying throughout the strand.

"Hold it!" From the opposite end of the strand came the loudest voice of all the bulbs. Uncle Flicker bellowed, "Let the boy talk. Give him time to tell the story."

"Thank you. I don't know how interesting it will be, but here goes."

His mom leaned sideways and touched him and whispered, "You will do fine, and you always make things interesting."

"Will you let the boy talk?"

"I was just encouraging him."

"Mom, Dad. It's okay. I'm encouraged. I'm ready to explain. Here's what happened."

There was not a sound from any of the bulbs when he began to speak. Bobby explained that there were still other words to learn and he hadn't completed the whole test. Then he started with the first word he had said for his test. He enunciated it very clearly. Then he would pause and say the word again. Within a few minutes he had spoken each of the words on the test he had been given. When he was finished he stopped and waited for some reaction. But there was only quiet, until he began to hear some light squeaking, which was much like human giggling. Then came cousin Flash's voice from the middle of the strand.

"That is hilarious. Say those words again."

"I'm glad you're liking this. Although it sounds like all of you think it is funny. I can hear you chuckling."

In the middle of the strand, Blinker bumped against Flash, smiled, squeaked for a moment, and then yelled back toward Bobby. "Everybody likes it. But you have to admit, it sounds funny when you say human words. Do the one again where you ask 'What is your name?'"

"Okay. Since I am so funny, this one is especially for you."

Even with the balcony door closed, the sound of voices and customers laughing could be heard from the new restaurant across the street. But that noise wasn't enough

to prevent the bulbs from hearing Bobby when he shouted proudly, "*Wuuuhht esss urr naahm?*"

The bulbs began to squeak, giggle, chuckle, and whatever other noise they could make, because it was so hard not to laugh.

"Go ahead and laugh at me," Bobby suddenly cried. "*It isn't easy learning human language. Do you think you could do any better?*"

"*Oh, don't get your feelings hurt, my wonderful son. We're not laughing at you; we are laughing at how different it sounds. All of our life we have heard the noise of human voices and not known what they were saying. Only you could interpret for us. But now when we hear you say it, we can actually hear a sound that at least makes a little sense to it.*" His mom looked directly at him and smiled. "*It is different and exciting, but it is funny too.*"

"*Yeah, Mom is right. We love hearing you, and we are proud of you, but it is still funny. Can't you understand that?*"

"Okay," Bobby answered Dimmer. "*I guess I understand what Mom is trying to tell me. So do you want me to repeat all the words one more time?*"

Aunt Glaring tilted sideways and whispered, "*Go ahead. You know you want to do it again, and we love hearing it.*"

"*Okay. You've heard 'Merry Christmas' and 'What's Your Name?' Do you want to know what time it is?*"

Bobby paused, but none of the bulbs replied. After a moment, he said, *"Well, do you?"*

Stretching forward in his pod, his dad looked at Bobby. *"I don't care what time it is right now. We've always known you could read the numbers on the clock."*

"That's not what I meant. I was talking about how to ask the question 'Do you want to know what time it is?'"

"Sure, let's hear it."

"Okay, all of you get ready to laugh at me again."

Aunt Glaring whispered once more, *"Oh my goodness, don't be so sensitive. It will be fine. We are proud of you whether we think it is funny or not."*

"Okay," he said. He leaned sideways and clanked against her side. *"Here goes."*

As the noise of humans laughing at the restaurant on the street below filtered through the closed balcony windows, it mixed with the joyous sounds of the bulbs as they enjoyed Bobby's replay of the test he had studied so hard for and had finally passed earlier in the day.

The clock near the front door chimed seven times. Remington's mom opened her eyes on the sixth one. She had been sound asleep for longer than the thirty-minute nap she had planned to take. She looked at her watch, which read seven o'clock. "I wonder where Richard is,"

she mumbled to herself as she rolled over onto her back and started to slide her legs off the bed. Just as she sat up, she heard weird sounds coming through the air vent at the top of the wall next to her side of the bed.

The noise sounded like a bunch of bees buzzing. It was the third time in the past month she had heard similar sounds. The previous two times, the noise came through the air vent in the kitchen. But this was the first time she had heard it in the bedroom. She felt a cold chill sweep over her body. This time, the noise was more than that squeaky sound she had heard before. She froze in place, and her feet dangled off the bed.

"Wuuuuhtt tiiiyum esss?"

It was the same squeaky voice she heard in the kitchen. "Wuuuuhtt tiiiyum esss?"

"That's enough," she screamed, and she jumped to her feet and quickly ran to the bedroom door. She flung it open and screamed into the hallway, "Richard, Remington, Maria. Where are you? Come here, please!"

She waited, and when no one answered, she screamed all three names again. This time, there was an answer. "What ees it, *señora*?" She heard Maria's footsteps running through the dining room, and at the same moment, she heard the front door open.

"Is something wrong? I heard Lisa scream just as I was unlocking the door."

"I hear too, *señor*," Maria said, as she looked over her shoulder and continued running down the hall toward the bedroom.

"Lisa, are you okay?"

Remington ran out of the kitchen and saw his dad running behind Maria. "Hey, Dad, what's wrong with Mom?"

He didn't have time to answer because at that moment, Lisa ran around the corner and nearly collided with Maria. "There you are," she said, and then she saw Remington and her husband.

"What is it, Lisa?"

"Oh, I just heard ... " She stopped, and then she blushed and started to laugh. "Hi, honey. I guess you are going to have a fun time laughing at me."

"What do you mean? What happened?"

"Well, dear," she said to her husband, "I thought I heard noises coming through the air vent."

She put her arms around his shoulders and gave him a hug and a quick kiss on the cheek. "I'm sure it was coming from Remington's room."

"Hearing noises again? This is the third time, honey."

"I know. The other two times I was in the kitchen."

"You okay, *señora*? You be able to eat my meel I fix for all of you?"

"Oh, yes, Maria. In fact, that is probably what I need. Except now it is not a surprise for Richard."

"What? You mean you have a surprise, Maria?"

"*Si, señor.* It is my thank-you for your present to send me to see my relatives in the north."

"Well, after this excitement, I guess we should be ready to eat. I'm glad I got home earlier than I expected."

"I know. You come too early. I need half of the one hour, and I be ready to surprise you. Come help me in the keeetchin, Remington."

"Okay, Maria, but I need to get something from my bedroom. I will be right back."

Remington rushed into his bedroom and went straight to the strand. He reached down near the end closest to him and grabbed the blue bulb, but he didn't unscrew it like he normally did.

"Bobby, I know I told you not to practice in the ball-room if anyone was in the kitchen, but I guess you are going to have to be quiet and not practice even in the bedroom. My mom just heard noises through the vent in her bedroom. It must have been you. She thinks she is going crazy. Were you squeaking those human words and practicing in here?"

He looked at Bobby and waited, but the bulb didn't move. So Remington asked the question again. This time, the bulb slightly moved forward and then slowly backward, and the strand shook gently. Remington stepped back and looked at the bulb. "I wonder if you meant 'Yes'?"

Bobby again moved forward and backward.

"Well, if you are practicing the words I have taught you, then be careful. You can't make noises up here unless you know no one is in the bedroom downstairs. Now, I have to go eat. Maria has fixed a special meal for us tonight. Just remember, my good buddy, be careful."

"Don't take forever brushing your teeth and please hurry up and put your pajamas on. It's way too late for you to be up. You should already be asleep with school tomorrow."

"I know, Mom, but you have to admit that it was worth it. That roasted duck Maria cooked was unbelievable."

"I hear you, Remington." Maria smiled as she walked in the room. "You really like that food I cook?"

"You bet," Remington said as he walked out of the bathroom brushing his teeth. "It was fantastic." Toothpaste started running down the front of his chin, and he quickly stepped back into the bathroom to wash his face. A few seconds later he looked at Maria and smiled.

"My folks and I must have told you at least ten times tonight how good it tasted. Right, Mom?"

"Yes we did and each time you would start blushing just like you are doing right now. But, I will say it again, it really was great."

"Thank you, *señora*. I glad you like eet. Eet ees special recipe from my mother many years ago."

Remington came back into the room. "See, Mom, I was quick."

"Yes, I see you put on a clean pair of pajamas. Now get in bed."

Remington crawled under the covers, but then he immediately started to get back out.

"What now?"

"I have to turn my lights on."

"Stay there, Remington. Maria, will you plug those lights in?"

"*Si, señora.*"

Remington's mom bent down and gave him a kiss and pulled the covers up under his chin. Then she turned and told Maria, "Let's go. He needs to get lots of sleep."

"Good night, Mom. Good night, Maria."

They both said good night, and Maria closed the door.

Remington lay there for at least two or three minutes. He just stared at the lighted strand on the windowsill. He never got tired of seeing the bulbs shine. Finally, when he was sure Maria and his mom had gone downstairs and it was quiet in the hallway outside the door, he got out of bed and walked to the windowsill. He could still hear noises from across the street. He peeked through the slats in the blinds that covered the window and saw people on the sidewalk in front of the restaurant.

Now, he turned back and looked at the bulbs. He went and stared for a moment at Bobby. "You have got to be more careful, Bobby. Don't practice in here, just like I told you, unless you know that no one is in my parent's bedroom. But I am not scolding you. I just want you to be cautious. I am proud you are trying to learn. Tomorrow, you get to try and say the words that mean how I feel about you."

8

More Lessons

A Birthday He Would Never Forget

Richard entered Remington's room and immediately walked over to the windowsill. He opened the balcony shutters slightly and peered down into the street below. It was quiet, and nobody was walking along the narrow sidewalks at seven thirty. That would change in the next thirty minutes.

He reached down and unplugged the Christmas tree lights.

"Are you sure you want to do that?" Remington's mom asked. "You know how he is about those lights. He'll want to turn them off."

At that moment, Remington rolled to his side and slowly opened his eyes. His dad reached down and plugged the bulbs back in.

"Hi, Dad. I'm getting up but please leave the lights on. This is the biggest day of my life."

"You mean we don't have to beg you to get out of bed today?" his mom asked.

"Of course not. I just told you, this is the biggest day of my life."

"Really?" His dad looked at him with a frown. "Why? What's important about today?"

"Dad, you're kidding, right?"

"About what? I know it's time you got ready for school."

"It's my *birthday*. How could you forget?"

Remington's mom and dad looked at each other, and then they began to laugh loudly. "Forget? We didn't forget, you goofy ten-year-old. Come on in, Maria." Remington's dad reached for the handle and pulled the door open. "Surprise!"

Maria hurried into the room, pushing a cart full of all kinds of fruit, tortas, eggs, bacon, and huge Spanish breakfast rolls, plus lots of fresh *jugo de naranja*.

> *Feliz cumpleanos a tu,*
> *Feliz cumpleanos a tu,*
> *Feliz cumpleanos mi pelirrojo,*
> *Feliz cumpleanos a tu.*

"Mom, how long did it take you to learn it?"

"I am smarter than you think. Maria taught it to me yesterday."

"Well, thanks, Mom, Dad, and Maria. Now do I really get to eat this breakfast in bed, just like a movie star?"

"Just like a movie star, buddy. Dig in and enjoy. I've got to get ready for work. But don't stay too long. You

need to be out of bed by eight so you will be ready to leave on time."

"Okay, Dad. Mom, you and Maria want to eat breakfast with me?"

"No, *niño*, I have work to do in the kitchen."

"I'll go help Maria, unless you want me to stay and talk with you while you eat."

"No, that's okay. I'll just enjoy my Christmas tree lights and my special breakfast."

"Okay, see you downstairs in half an hour," she said and closed the door. She stood there for a moment. "Christmas tree lights on March first. I'll never understand."

Remington chewed slowly on his bacon. He took a big gulp of orange juice and nibbled on some eggs. Mostly, he just stared at the bulbs on the windowsill and made sure he had saved enough room for his favorite part of his birthday breakfast. He took a huge bite out of the creamy *torta* Maria had baked, and with part of the pastry clinging to his chin, he slid out of bed and walked across the room. He looked down at his special blue bulb.

"Do you realize I'm now a 'double-digit kid'?" Not expecting an answer, he started to explain but never got a chance. Even though it wasn't the first time he had seen Bobby answer 'yes' to a question by moving forward and backward, it still surprised him. His mouth flew open and he nearly dropped the pastry. "That's just like you did the other day. You're saying 'yes' again.

"I've seen you escape from your socket. I've seen you fly into the air and disappear, and fly back to me, plus lots of other tricks, but moving back and forth in your socket when you answer 'yes' is so neat."

Remington continued to stare at the bulb, but when there was no further movement he took a final bite of his *torta* and started to walk away. However, he was surprised one more time when Bobby suddenly tilted himself into the straight-up sitting position and started moving again. "Oh, my gosh! Did you know this is my birthday? Is this a special present to me, Bobby? Is that why you are moving back and forth repeatedly?"

Bobby beamed with excitement. "*He understands me. Can you believe it? He knows it's my way of saying 'yes.'*"

"*That's fine, but are you going to sing 'Happy Birthday' to him in Bulbese?*"

"*Give me time,*" he answered his brother. "*I can't do everything at once.*"

"*Well, if you really want to impress him, show him how we say 'no.'*"

He looked past his mom and nodded to his dad. "*Good idea because that's what I have to tell him right now.*"

Remington was so happy. Bobby had actually given him a birthday present. But now he had to hurry and get ready for school. As he walked towards the bathroom, he looked back across the room. When he did, he was surprised once more.

Remington saw Bobby, still attached to his socket, move from a flat position into a sitting-up position just as he had done a couple of minutes ago. However, this time, instead of moving forward and backward, Bobby began to shake violently from side to side and continued to do so for another three or four seconds. Then, still tightly attached to his pod, he fell back down onto the windowsill.

"That must mean 'no,'" Remington squealed. "Oh, my gosh; my birthday present is getting better. I can't believe this is happening. Thank you very much, Bobby. Do you have anymore birthday surprises for me?"

The blue bulb quickly sat up again and moved forward and backward a couple of times. Remington started to ask another question but was interrupted by the voice of his mom. She was in the living room at the foot of the stairs.

"Remington McGillicuddy. What are you doing? Get down here. Daddy is waiting."

He raced into the bathroom, threw on his clothes, and didn't even take time to brush his teeth. He hurried toward the doorway but suddenly skidded to a stop. He raced back to the windowsill and unplugged the bulbs. He looked at Bobby. "I can't wait until after school. Do you really have another surprise?" He didn't have time to wait and see if the bulb would sit up and move forward again. He hurried out of the room.

"*Oh, if you only knew, Remington.*" Then, Bobby explained to the bulbs that all of them were going to be part of Remington's surprise when he got home from school.

B-e-e-e-p de, b-e-e-e-p de, beep-beep

The entire strand of bulbs now moved in unison and sat up straight.

Be-e-e-p de, b-e-e-e-p de, beep-beep

And then they tilted themselves forward in unison.

Be-e-e-p de, b-e-e-e-p de, beep-beep

Then they moved themselves back into a straight-up position, and as they all fell backward together, they shouted *beep, beep!*

For the first time, after so many tries, the song had sounded perfect. At least most of the bulbs thought so,

and each of them twisted and looked toward Bobby to see if he agreed.

Then Bobby tilted forward and said, *"It was perfect. It may have taken five hours of practice, but we have finally done it right."*

Downstairs in the first-floor bedroom, Remington's mom sat on the edge of the bed. She had just awakened from an afternoon *siesta*. "What's wrong with me?" she muttered. Tears formed in her eyes, and she stared into space. "I'm almost sure I wasn't dreaming. I swear that noise sounded like a song, but I've never heard anything like it. All that squeaky noise." She reached for a tissue on the nightstand and wiped her eyes. "And here I am talking to myself." Then she shouted, "Am I going crazy?"

Seconds later, the bedroom door flew open. Maria rushed into the room. "*¿Senora? Que tal?*"

She stared at the Nanny without saying anything.

"Are you okay, *senora?*"

Remington's mom shook her head and blinked her eyes. "Uh, yes, I'm okay, Maria. It must have been a bad dream."

"Well, eet is time you wake up. Remington will be home in an hour, and we need to geet all the party geefts up to the beeeg room."

"You are right. We have a lot to do." *Right now I'd do anything to help me get my mind off that squeaky noise.*

There had been more people at his Christmas party three months ago, but there were still at least twenty of Remington's classmates here today to enjoy his tenth birthday party. His mom and dad, and Maria, along with Juan and Anna, who managed the apartment building, also joined in the fun.

Remington had already received the surprise gift from Bobby, but he was still in for one more surprise. The doorbell rang, and Remington's mom went to the door to see who was there. At that moment, all of the children were following Remington's dad upstairs to the ballroom where the acrobats were going to put on their show.

"Remington, there are some people here to see you. I think you'll be happy to see them."

Remington was about halfway up the stairs between the first and second floor when he heard his mom. "You go on, Jacobi."

"Okay, Remingtone. I see you in the beeg ballroom."

Remington skipped down the stairs and hurried to the door. He heard a woman's voice say, "Thank you for asking them, and girls, I will be back to pick you up later."

Then he saw her. Grace Starr. *Oh, my goodness. She said she couldn't come, and Aaron and Christopher told me she said she didn't like me.*

"Hi, Remington."

He gulped before he spoke. "Uh, hi, Grace." *Boy, does she ever look great in that yellow dress. She looks like a star.* "I didn't think you could come to the party. You told me you had something else to do."

"I did," she said. "But I changed my mind. You met Elaine before, right?"

"Oh, hi, Elaine. I didn't know you were coming too."

"Remington! Where are your manners? We are very glad you came, Elaine. This is good because you know Aaron Bolwerk was the only fourth-grader here. Now he has someone else here from his class. That's nice."

The two girls looked at each other and giggled.

"What's so funny?" Remington asked.

"Elaine likes Aaron and hopes they can talk while she is here."

"Grace, don't say that."

"Well, it's true."

"Well, how about you? You said you wanted to see Remington."

"Elaine!"

"Girls, it's okay. We are glad you are here no matter what the reason. Now, Remington, take the girls upstairs before all of you miss the acrobats."

"Acrobats? Who are the acrobats?"

"Oh, wait until you see them. They were here at Christmas, and they were magnificent."

Remington's mom watched the three of them march up the stairs. *My son is growing up too fast.*

Remington received lots of presents and neat gifts at his party, but none better than his dad's surprise. He had brought back the same midget acrobats who had been the stars at his Christmas party, and today, they were even greater than they had been in December.

Their sometimes dangerous balancing and tumbling acts were so great that the children wouldn't let them stop. They kept applauding and applauding, and each time they tried to stop, the applause would get louder. By the time they finally left the ballroom floor, their one-hour performance had turned into a two-hour show.

When nine o'clock arrived, everyone had eaten lots of good food and played plenty of games and had enjoyed what everyone was calling the "double-digit" party. Parents began arriving to pick up their children, and those who remained were milling around the kitchen hoping to get one more piece of the birthday cake. Remington had just walked Grace to the door and thanked her for coming. Now was the perfect time for him to show his good friend Jacobi a surprise. He took his hand and pulled him out of the kitchen. They hurried up the stairs to the second floor.

"*¿Que pasa,* Remingtone?"

Remington loved the way Jacobi pronounced his name with the accent on *tone.*

"I have a surprise," he said to the eight-year-old son of one of the embassy guards. "You've become my best friend since my Christmas party, Jacobi, and I want you to see something no one has ever seen."

They walked into the bedroom, and Remington said, "See my Christmas tree lights?"

"*Porsupuesto.* I have seen them at your party, and the last time I came here to play."

"I know. I mean do you see anything different about them now?"

Jacobi walked to the windowsill. He bent over and peered closely at the bulbs. Then he straightened up and looked at Remington. "No, I see nothing deeeferent."

"Well get ready for a big surprise. You are about to see something very different. Step back." He pushed Jacobi a few feet away from the windowsill. "You've got to believe what I tell you, but first watch what happens when I speak to the blue bulb next to the end of the cord."

"*Are you sure you should do this?*" Bobby's mom whispered to him.

Bobby glanced at her, taking in her worried expression. "I've got to. It's the only way he will truly believe, once and for all, that this is how we say, 'yes.' Plus, it won't be nearly as big a deal in a few minutes when we surprise him and sing 'Happy Birthday.'"

His mom sighed. "Okay, dear, go ahead."

"So what is supposed to happen, Remingtone?" Jacobi watched the strand with obvious doubt. "You want me to believe these bulbs can say 'yes' and 'no'?"

"Trust me, Jacobi. I know it sounds weird, but be patient. Here we go. One more time."

Then Remington turned away from Jacobi and again leaned in close to the blue bulb. "Come on, aren't you glad I had a good time at my party?"

Remington had barely gotten the words out of his mouth when he screamed in delight, and Jacobi screamed in fright.

"Go for it," said Aunt Glaring.

"I am," said Bobby, and he whispered. "Puhrumba! Puhrumba! Puhrumba!" Then he began to move upward. "I'm doing it!" He tilted himself straight up and moved forward and backward two or three times.

Jacobi jumped backward, keeping his eyes on the moving bulb. "Increible! Da miedo! ¿Es un fantasma?"

Remington laughed. "No, he's not a ghost, and don't be scared. He is just a real magical bulb. His name is Bobby, and I have taught him how to say some words in English."

"*No, me digas, Remingtone.* I don't believe you. *No me tomes el pelo.*"

"It is the truth, and I am not pulling your leg. This is Bobby's gift to me for my birthday. He can also say 'no' when he shakes sideways."

"Remingtone, you are my friend, but I can't beeeleeve theees goofy things."

"Just watch, Jacobi."

But he couldn't. He was too frightened, and he raced out of the room.

Remington chased him and caught him at the bottom of the stairs. He could see he was crying. "Don't tell anyone. This is our secret."

"Remington?" his mom's voice came from outside the front door in the hallway. "Jacobi's folks are waiting to take him home."

In between sobs, Jacobi whispered, "Don't worry. I tell no one."

"Well, wipe the tears from your face so your folks aren't worried. Promise me you mean it; you won't tell anyone."

Jacobi stared at his friend and then crossed his heart with his right index finger. "I promise. I too scared. *¡Es una fantasma!*"

"No. Not a ghost," he said, as he watched his friend go out the front door with his parents. "Just a fantastic little Christmas tree light bulb."

But even Remington had no idea how fantastic Bobby Bright and his family were about to become.

Maria and Remington's mom had cleaned up almost everything. It was after ten o'clock, and Remington's dad was working upstairs in the ballroom. "You get to bed, Remington. Maria and I have some more dishes to wash in the kitchen. Did you get your homework done?"

"I didn't have much, Mom. I think the teachers knew it was my birthday."

"Oh, Remington." His mom laughed. "I know you think you are important but not that important. Teachers don't give homework assignments based on birthdays."

"All right, well, I'm going to bed. Good night, Mom. Good night, Maria."

"*Buenas noches*, Remington, *y una vez maz, feliz cumpleanos.*"

"Thanks, Maria, I liked that extra 'Happy Birthday.'"

Remington took the steps two at a time to the landing and turned toward his room. Just as he started to open the bedroom door, he heard a sound. His hand tightly

gripped the handle, and he leaned against the door to listen. It was a noise he had never heard before.

He swung the door open and looked into the room. He could see the Christmas tree lights on the windowsill. They were shining just as they had been an hour ago when Jacobi was with him.

He decided to check the balcony doors, and he quickly walked across the room. They were locked like they were supposed to be. *Surely*, he thought, *the noise didn't come from the restaurant across the street.*

He turned back around, and when he did, he received the most surprising birthday gift he had ever gotten—and one he would remember forever.

B-e-e-e-p de, b-e-e-e-p de, beep-beep
The entire strand of bulbs now moved in unison and sat up straight.

Be-e-e-p de, b-e-e-e-p de, beep-beep
And then they tilted themselves forward in unison.

Be-e-e-p de, b-e-e-e-p de, beep-beep
Then they moved themselves back into a straight-up position, and as they all fell backward together, they shouted *beep, beep!*

He just stood there in disbelief. Even though he had just heard it, he knew no one else would ever believe this

story. Well, maybe granddad would, but certainly no one else.

He just knew it couldn't be anything else but the happy birthday song. "That was happy birthday in Bulbese, wasn't it, Bobby?"

It took only a brief moment for the blue bulb to sit back up straight and tilt forward.

"Yes," Remington shouted. "Oh, my gosh. This makes my double-digit birthday even greater."

Remington heard his dad's footsteps coming up the stairs from the first floor. He leaned down and whispered to Bobby, "This is so exciting. I want to learn Bulbese like you learned some human words. Can I learn the same things you learned from me?"

Aunt Glaring leaned over to tap Bobby urgently. *"Hurry, I hear footsteps outside the door."*

"Okay. Let me tell him 'yes.'" Bobby tilted forward one more time before falling back down.

"Just in the nick of time," whispered his mom. *"The door is opening."*

The door opened, and Remington's dad looked at him. "Did you call for me or yell something? I thought I heard you when I was on the stairs."

"Yeah, Dad, sorry. It was me. I just had such a great tenth birthday. I just felt like shouting. Thanks for a marvelous day," and he ran and leaped into his father's arms. As he hugged him, he thought to himself, *That*

wasn't really a lie, maybe a little fib. After all, I did have the greatest birthday ever, even if my amazing bulbs were the main reason.

9

Bobby, the Professor

Bobby had always believed that Remington was a very smart little boy. He still wanted to believe it, but he couldn't understand why he couldn't speak Bulbese any better than he did.

For the last two weeks since Remington's birthday, Bobby had spent every afternoon in the upstairs ballroom after school, and on Saturday and Sunday mornings in Remington's bedroom, trying to teach him just one little phrase. Bobby remembered it had been very difficult for him to learn some human words. But he thought he had at least managed to say something after two or three days.

Remington wasn't making any progress, and Bobby thought, '*What's your name?*' should be one of the easiest things to say in Bulbese.

Yesterday morning, Remington had actually started crying because he still couldn't say it right.

"I don't understand how something as easy as *beep. ... uhh. ... de' ... beep, beep* is so hard to say."

"*You have to have patience, Bobby,*" his mom scolded him. "*Give Remington a chance.*"

"A chance, Mom? At this rate, the McGillicuddys will have taken us back to America, and he won't know five phrases."

"Oh, Dimmer, be nice. Your brother doesn't need any help from you when it comes to disagreeing with me."

"Hey, you both are wrong. I have patience. I think I just need to teach him something easier. After I do that, then we can go back to 'What's your name?'"

"*Good idea!*" bellowed Uncle Flicker from the opposite end of the strand. "*I'm tired of hearing him mumble and mumble and never saying it correctly.*"

Bobby started to tell him it was still a lot easier to listen than to teach him, but just then, the bedroom door flung open, and Remington ran into the room.

"School got out an hour early today, and I think it means good luck." He reached down and unscrewed Bobby, turned on the strand of lights, and walked out of the room with the blue bulb in his hand.

He picked up his backpack, which was sitting in the hallway, and headed up the stairs to the ballroom. As he hit the third-floor landing, he put Bobby directly in front of him and said, "Don't worry. I practiced all the way home from school. I sat in the back of the car because both Mom and Dad picked me up today. I whispered the whole time they were talking, and I practiced and practiced. Just you listen, Bobby."

Remington wasn't angry with Maria, but he wished she hadn't spoiled everything. Just as he had started to say 'What's your name?' in Bulbese, she had walked into the ballroom.

"There is no Spanish lesson today, Remingtone, unless we have time after dinner. I must go shopping right now at *El Corte Ingles*. We need *comestibles*."

"You mean groceries."

"Yes, that is what I mean. That is a difficult word. I trouble saying it."

Remington smiled. *I sure know what you mean about difficult words.*

"I see you later then, Remingtone?" She smiled and walked toward the doorway.

"Wait a second. I will walk downstairs with you. I want some *jugo de naranja*."

Remington hurried into the kitchen when he got to the first floor. Two minutes later he heard Maria close the front door. He took his glass of orange juice and headed back toward the staircase. He passed the hall to his parents' bedroom and he shouted to his mother, "I'll be upstairs studying."

When he reached the ballroom, he opened the door and went immediately to the table. He sat the orange

juice down and picked up the blue bulb and held it close. "Listen to this," he said.

"*It was unbelievable.*" Bobby was back in his socket, and Remington was having dinner downstairs. "*Just like that, he said it. He sounded like he had been speaking Bulbese forever. I couldn't believe it.*"

"*You mean after all that whining and moaning you did about him not being able to do it, he just up and said it?*"

"*That's exactly what I mean. You would have been proud of him my little sister. Beep. ... uh ... de ... beep? Everything was just right. His timing was perfect, which all of you know is the key to our language, and so was his inflection. I can assure you I was shocked.*"

"*Well, did you get a chance to teach him anything else, or were you too flabbergasted to go on?*"

Bobby looked at the pod four sockets to his right. It was always easy to see Sparkle because she hung right on the edge of the windowsill. Bobby could see her easily.

"*Good question. The answer is 'yes' and 'no.' Yes, I did teach him something else, and no, I wasn't totally surprised. Once he could say one phrase I thought he would get better. In fact it only took him about three tries.*"

"*What was it?*" shouted Uncle Glimmer from the middle of the strand, "*What was the next one?*"

"Well, when I nodded back and forth so he would know he had finally said 'What's your name?' correctly, he squealed and started jumping up and down. So I thought, if he is this happy, I'll see if he understands. I rolled up into a sitting position and said, 'B-e-e-e-e-e-e-p. Beep... beep?'

"He looked at me with a strange expression, and then surprised me even more. This was obviously a special day for both of us, because he immediately said, 'Do you mean, am I happy?' I nodded forward and backward, and five minutes later, he was asking, 'Are you happy?' in Bulbese. It was like he had been saying it all his life.

B-e-e-e-e-e-e-p. Beep... beep?"

"What do you think caused this sudden ability to finally learn?"

He turned to Aunt Glaring. "I really think it must have been his friend, Jacobi. Remember the little guy we scared after the birthday party? Well, Remington said Jacobi had been so frightened by what he had seen that day that he had hardly spoken to Remington in the past two weeks.

"But Jacobi came up to Remington today and told him he had decided that maybe that bulb was magical. Remington told Jacobi that he was trying to learn some of our language. It was then that Jacobi told Remington that he would help him if he needed it because he knew how difficult it was to learn a foreign language."

"But why did that help Remington?"

Bobby felt like he was watching a tennis match, turning back and forth between Sparkle, Aunt Glaring, and now his mom. "I think Remington knew right then that his eight-year-old friend was smarter than he was, and Remington decided he should learn some Bulbese real quickly.

"Whatever it was, it must have worked because we were practicing how to say 'What time is it?' when he finally had to go eat dinner."

"I think I would call this a good day's work, and you deserve your first applause as a true professor."

As the bulbs clapped their filaments in unison, Bobby waved one of his at his dad and said, "Thanks."

10

Remington's Final Exam

Six weeks of work was over. Remington was finally ready to take the final exam on the ten phrases he had learned in Bulbese. It made him think about earlier in the year when he had given Bobby his final test.

He was practicing alone in the upstairs ballroom. Tomorrow was Saturday, and his mom and dad would be out of town most of the day on a short business trip his dad needed to take. Maria would be with him, but she was going to be busy preparing a big meal for some of dad's coworkers at the embassy who were coming to dinner that evening.

Remington knew he would have plenty of time alone to take the test. He was excited.

He finished buttoning his shirt as he walked out of the bathroom and came to the windowsill. He walked over to the balcony doors and swung them open and stepped

outside. Sunlight poured over his shoulders into the room. It was nine thirty and a beautiful mid-May Saturday morning in Madrid. The tiny restaurant across the street had lots of people already there, drinking coffee or having a pastry to start the day. He stood there for a moment and looked down at those who were sitting at tables outside before he turned around and came back inside. He walked to the windowsill and pulled the plug from the wall. Then he waited for the bulbs to cool off before he unscrewed the blue one in front and picked it up.

"Today is my big day, Bobby. Let's go do it after I have some breakfast."

"Do what, Remington?"

Remington slid the bulb into his pocket and turned around. He saw her standing in the doorway. "Uh, nothing, Mom. Just mumbling to myself about tests and exams. I'm going to go study right after breakfast and get most of my weekend homework over early. It's hard to believe there are only three more weeks of school. Mom, I thought you and Dad were leaving early?"

"We got delayed, but we are going now. We will still be back in time for supper at eight o'clock tonight. You mind Maria and stay out of trouble."

"I always do, Mom."

"Well, good for you," she said and turned to leave, but then she suddenly wheeled around and looked at her son,

who was looking out the balcony window. "You may think I don't know, but I do, Remington. I hear you talking to that bulb all the time. The noise comes right through the air vent. I was frightened for a while, but now I know I'm not hearing weird sounds. It's just you."

"Oh, you are definitely right, Mom. It was me, and I hope I didn't scare you."

He turned around, but his mother was gone. He could already hear her steps on the stairs.

The exam was already two hours in. "Five down, five more phrases to go," said Remington. He sounded like he was proud of himself.

Bobby thought otherwise. He thought the test would have been over by now. It was sure taking Remington a long time, but at least after numerous attempts he had gotten the first five correct.

There were five more to go:

> What time is it?
> Do you like school?
> I love you.
> Happy Birthday.
> Let's play a game.

"What time is it? Right, Bobby? That's what you want me to say?"

Bobby tilted forward and backward. Remington did what he did with each phrase. He wrote it down in English, and then after he had passed the test, he tried to write it down in Bulbese, which was really tough to do; and then of course, he had to pronounce all the beeps and pauses, and that was really, really difficult.

Finally, almost three hours later, Remington stood up and walked away from the ballroom desk. He headed downstairs. He was thirsty and exhausted, but he was finished.

Earlier in the year when Remington had given Bobby his final exam, he had to grade him and give him his final score. He knew that Bobby was going to have to do the same to him. Although Remington certainly had no idea how Bobby was going to actually let him know since he couldn't say any of those things in English and he certainly couldn't write them down.

"Well, that's your problem, Bobby," Remington mumbled to himself as he headed down the stairs to the first floor. "I'm too tired and too thirsty to worry about it."

"So how did you finally give him his grades, Bobby?"

Bobby turned to face Aunt Glaring. *"It was one of the best things I've ever done in my life."*

When he didn't say anything for a few seconds, she leaned over toward him and said, *"Quit being so mysterious. Tell us."*

"While Remington was downstairs getting something to drink, I suddenly figured it out. I yelled 'puhrumba' five times instead of three and lifted off the desk. When I looked down, I saw an inkpad lying next to the lamp. It was nearly hidden, and I hadn't seen it earlier. I had watched Remington one night take a tiny little object and put it on the pad, and then he would take it and stamp something on his homework. I decided to try it and see if it would work for me because I knew it was kind of wet. So, I just dropped down on it. Then I spun back up in the air and landed right next to the first phrase on the test, which was 'Merry Christmas.' Remington had said it the best out of all the things he had said. So I touched the paper and left a dot, and then I kept repeating what I had done. I went back to the pad and then back to the test until I had put four dots on the paper."

Twinkle frowned. *"What did that mean, Bobby?"*

"It meant I had given him the highest grade. I had heard Remington talk about a four-point grade average in school and that it meant he had all As, which is something teachers give students when they do good in their studies."

"So, did you give him four dots for every phrase?"

"No way." He turned to his other sister. "I am proud to say that I graded very fairly even though he is my friend. I gave him one other four-dot grade, and all the rest were three-dot scores except for a pair of two-dot grades."

"What were they? It sounds like he didn't do very good in those."

"Are you worried about low grades? You're a bulb mom sounding like a human mom. He had lots of trouble saying, 'Do you like school?' and 'What time is it?'"

"You said he got two four-dots. What was the other?"

Bobby looked at his mother. "You know Dad has sure been asking a lot of questions lately. I think he must be feeling much better." Then he looked past his mom and saw his dad smiling. "The other phrase he really said well was 'Let's play a game.'"

His dad grinned. "Well, it sounds to me like you've had enough of being a professor."

"You're right. I am worn out. I don't think I want to ever be a professor again, but I do admit it was fun for a while."

"So, I guess you'd rather be a student than a professor, huh?" The question came from the middle of the strand where he saw his cousin Energizer waving one of his filaments.

"You are right about that."

"Guess what?" said his ornery cousin. "I don't want to be either."

Some of the bulbs started laughing, and then Blinker yelled from the opposite end of the strand. "That's no surprise. You couldn't pass a test whether you were a teacher or a student."

Flicker scolded his son. "Why would you say something like that about Energizer?"

"Because it's Energizer."

Then every bulb on the strand laughed.

"It's okay," said Dazzling, who was just a couple of sockets from Energizer. "Everybody loves a dummy."

11

School Is Almost Over

The door between the kitchen and dining room swung open. His mom walked in. "Good morning!"

When he didn't answer, she asked, "What are you thinking about, Remington McGillicuddy? You have a worrisome look on your face."

"Oh, hi, Mom. What do you mean?"

"Well, it's Saturday of the final weekend of school, and you are sitting here in the kitchen looking like you have lost your best friend or your best video game."

Remington didn't answer but instead took a big drink of orange juice. "Boy, this is the best *jugo de naranja* I've had since we moved to Spain." He wiped some of the juice off his lips.

"Your daddy and I love it too. Maria found it at a tiny little shop two blocks from here. It's a special brand. You can't buy it at *El Corte Ingles* or any of the other big supermarkets. Maria says it is made in Northern Spain, close to the town where she used to live. She thinks only a few small stores sell it."

"Will she get some more?"

"Whenever she can find it in that small grocery store. But enough about that. What were you so deep in thought about when I came into the room?"

"Just worried about my two final exams on Monday and Tuesday."

"Well, you have As in both classes. You should do fine. Just make sure you study some more tomorrow.

"Do you want to go see a movie later this morning? Remember it's just you and me today. Maria tiptoed into your room real early this morning and gave you a kiss. Then we took her to *Atocha*, and she left on the five-o'clock train. She was so excited about the trip we gave her for her birthday."

"I know, Mom. She came in and gave me a kiss after you had tucked me in to bed. She said she would miss me this week."

"This is a great moment for her, Remington. She is going back to her hometown to see lots of her relatives. Many of them won't even know she is still alive. It will be a very special few days for her. So, how about us?

"Daddy is working the weekend shift at the embassy. You know the big theatre on *Gran Via* that sometimes has movies in English? Well, it is showing a children's movie today called *Brother Bear*. Do you happen to remember me telling you that Daddy's second cousins, Dan and Troy, were animated artists who used to work in Hollywood, and this is one of the movies they worked on?"

"Really? You mean they helped draw the characters?"

"That's right. Anyway, it is even better because for some strange reason it is in English without Spanish translation, although there are Spanish subtitles. So, what do you think? Should we go?"

Remington finished his orange juice and stared into the empty glass for a few seconds. Just as he was about to answer, his mom said, "Are you sure everything is okay with you?"

"Sure, I'm fine. I was just thinking maybe we could wait and go to the late-afternoon show?"

"Well, I guess we could. What are you going to do this morning?"

"I really want to study some for my final exams so I can get part of it out of the way before doing the rest tomorrow."

"So you are really ready to do homework right after breakfast?"

"I know it's not like me. Maybe I'm changing since I am ten years old."

She smiled and chuckled. "Oh, I think without question that's probably it. Go on, get it over with, and then the movies later."

Remington hurried to his bedroom and collected Bobby off the strand. This had become a Saturday morning ritual for the past three weeks since he had taken his final exam.

"This is fun," said Remington, "practicing these ten phrases with each other."

He sat down on the edge of the bed and placed the blue bulb on a pillow. "Go ahead, Bobby. I've got just over three hours until lunch. My mom and I are going to a movie this afternoon. Let's start today with 'Merry Christmas.' I never get tired of saying, 'Merry Christmas.'"

But before Remington had a chance to begin, Bobby rose into a sitting position and shook his body from side to side.

"Hey, what's wrong?"

"*Beep... uh. ... de'... beep?*"

Remington stared at the bulb for a few seconds, and then realized. "Oh, okay. You want to start with 'what's your name?' Okay. My name is Remington. See, I answered you like I should have."

Bobby tilted back and forth three or four times. It was his way of telling Remington he had done very well.

A wide grin spread across Remington's face. "Thank you. And now I will ask you. Okay, here goes. *Beep... uh ... de'... beep?*"

Remington always remembered the first time he had ever heard that squeaky voice. It had now been over two and a half years. Then he had only heard it twice until they had started teaching each other different words and phrases. He always was eager to hear the tiny little

sound coming from his buddy. The blue bulb rolled to its side and squeaked, "Baabee."

"You understood me." Remington giggled. "You know, no matter how many times we do this, it is always fun."

Bobby moved forward and backward again. He agreed.

"Okay. Let's do another one. Remington looked down at the bulb and said, "Beep-duh, beep, beep." Remington waited for Bobby to answer, but when nothing happened, he repeated the phrase again.

Again, there was no sound from the bulb. Remington frowned for the slightest moment but suddenly a smile crept across his face. "Okay. I think I know. I said it too fast, right? I remember. You have to pause just right to say 'Merry Christmas' in Bulbese. Okay, here I go again." Remington took a deep breath and then said, "Beep... duh'... beep, beep."

Bobby quickly tilted forward and backward three or four times, and his little voice squeaked.

"I'm glad you liked it," said Remington, "but now it is your turn. The way you say it is so cute and funny that it gives me goose bumps."

Remington waited a moment and looked at the bulb. When he heard nothing, he said, "Go ahead. Say it." Then he stared once more at Bobby and this time he didn't have to wait long.

A couple of seconds later he felt the goose bumps rise on his arms and he heard, "Murryy... Creesmuss."

And that's the way their Saturday morning session went, exchanging roles as professor and student and enjoying the good times. Finally they heard a voice from downstairs. "Remington, it's time for lunch. This is the third time I've called you. Get down here."

Remington stuck his head out of his bedroom doorway. "I'm coming, Mom. I need to wash my hands." Then he ducked back in the room and closed the door.

"This was fun again, Bobby. I'm better, but I still can't say 'What time is it?' and 'Do you like school?' very well." He picked the bulb up and walked to the strand and screwed it back in its socket. He looked at the strand of bulbs. "I can't turn you on right now. We are going to a movie this afternoon. Good-bye," and he raced out of the room.

When he reached the kitchen, he smiled at his mom and said, "I studied real hard this morning. I deserve a chance to relax. I'm looking forward to *Brother Bear*."

That's not really a lie. I did study. It was just Bulbese.

12

The Grandparents Are Back in Spain

Mr. McGillicuddy hung two pair of slacks in the closet and then checked to make sure everything else was out of his suitcase. He turned off the light and left the bedroom to join Mrs. McGillicuddy. She was downstairs visiting with Maria in the kitchen.

He walked down the stairs to the second floor landing, and as he turned to start on down to the first floor, he heard a noise from Remington's bedroom. He walked over to the door and knocked. "Remington, are you in there?"

He waited a moment and then the door swung open. "Hi, Grandpa."

"I thought I heard you talking in here?"

"I was." Remington turned his head and looked to the opposite side of the room where the balcony doors stood open.

Mr. McGillicuddy could see the windowsill next to them, and he noticed the strand of lights. "So, there they are—the famous Christmas bulbs. Have you enjoyed your lights all these months?"

"Oh, very much, and I am very happy you left them for me, Grandpa. That was a great idea you had last January."

"You going to tell me what that noise was?"

"Uh...sure...I guess." Remington walked out into the hallway, and to make sure no one was nearby, he took a few steps to the top of the staircase and peered down into the living room below. Then he hurried back inside and closed the door.

"What was that all about?"

"Grandpa. You have to keep this a secret."

"Were you talking to those bulbs?" A smile broke across his face, and he started laughing and picked up his grandson. "Give me a hug and tell me, were you?"

Remington wrapped his arms around his grandfather's neck and squeezed as hard as he could.

"Whoa! You are too strong for me. I'm going to put you down. Let loose of me, please."

Remington kept squeezing and hugging.

"Come on, old buddy. Let go."

"Okay, Grandpa." He released his grip and slid out of his grandfather's arms to the floor. "I'm sure glad you and Grandma are here. We are going to take a great trip in a few days. You know we are going back to *Morella* and *Peñiscola* again because all of us liked those towns so much last December. And, we are also going to see some different places too. We're going to a jazz festival that Mom and Dad want to go see. I don't know if I will like it."

"Oh, it will be fun, and it will be good for you to enjoy some different types of music. Who knows, you might like it a lot. And I'm sure we will have a great time wherever we go, but you still haven't answered my question. Were you talking to those bulbs?"

"Well, if I'm going to tell you…" Remington looked up at his grandfather, and he had both of his hands closed in a fist and pinned against his hips.

"Wow! You look like you are angry with me. What did I do?"

"Just want you to know that this is not a laughing matter." He paused and kept staring at his grandfather.

"Wow. You are growing up, my ten-year-old buddy. That's something adults normally say. So, what is not a laughing matter?"

"Well, I have been sitting here for the last half hour while you and Grandma were getting your clothes unpacked. My buddy, Bobby, hasn't spoken to me, not a single word all day long."

Mr. McGillicuddy raised his eyebrows, which he was very good at, and always looked funny when he did. "Whoa! You're telling me you think that blue bulb talks to you?"

"Come on, Grandpa, you know he's magical. Believe me! And since you and Grandma were here, I have even taught him some human words, and he has taught me some *Bulbese*."

"Wait a minute," interrupted Mr. McGillicuddy. "Did you just say *Bulbese?*"

"Yes, that's what you said you thought the bulbs would speak if they could. Remember you said it just before you left to go home in January?"

"Oh, I do remember. We all had a big laugh about it."

"Well, there is nothing funny about it. It's the truth."

"I know your bulbs are special, but please don't tell me they can also talk."

"No, only Bobby, but today he hasn't said a word to me."

"Come on, Remington, you are kidding me, right?"

"No, I am not kidding. It is true. About a month after you and Grandma went back to America, we started teaching each other."

"You! You started teaching a bulb to speak?"

"Yes, and he started teaching me."

"Remington, I believe in your bulbs more than anyone in this family because I have seen things the others haven't, but you surely don't expect me to believe you are talking in bulb language."

Mr. McGillicuddy didn't give his grandson time to answer. Instead, he just kept talking. "You know, when you reminded me a few seconds ago about what I had said. I remembered all of you laughed at me. And there was reason to laugh, because when I said the word *Bulbese,* I was joking."

"Yes, you were, and I laughed at you too. But it is no longer a joke, Grandpa, because a month later, I learned from Bobby that was the name of their language. He actually squeaked it to me."

"What do you mean 'squeaked'?"

"When he talks, it sounds like a person's voice squeaking."

"Oh, my gosh, Remington. You keep talking like this, and I may believe you." He paused for a moment, a frown stretched across his face. "Oh, what am I saying? Of course, I don't mean that. I can't believe I'm even saying or thinking this." Then, the frown turned into a big smile.

"I know that look on your face, Grandpa. I see it from Mom and Dad all the time, although they don't smile. They just frown at me like they don't believe me. But you have seen enough to know I'm telling the truth." Remington stood up on his tiptoes and looked up into his grandfather's eyes. "This time, you better believe me because it is true. Here, let me show you." Remington pulled on his grandfather's right arm. "Bend down here." When Mr. McGillicuddy did, Remington said, "*Beep, b-e-e-e-e-e-e-e-e-e-e-p, b-e-e-e-p.*"

Mr. McGillicuddy's eyes opened wide, and his eyebrows raised up so high they looked like they might jump right off his forehead. Remington quickly repeated the Bulbese words again.

"Oh, brother! What are you saying?"

"I just told you that I love you."

Mr. McGillicuddy lowered his voice, bent over, and looked Remington in the face. He whispered, "You did. You mean that is *Bulbese?*"

"That is *Bulbese,* and that is how it sounds. It's a bunch of beeps. I mean I only know a few things. I can say Merry Christmas and—"

"What's that noise in there?" There was a knock on the door.

"Quiet. It's Grandma."

"Don't worry," Mr. McGillicuddy said. "I'm in too much shock to do or say anything."

Just then, the door swung open. "What's going on in here with you two?"

"Oh, hi, Grandma. Just us boys talking."

"Well, how about you boys come downstairs. Maria is so excited we are back in Spain that she baked those *tortas* you like so much, Remington."

"Well, I like them too."

"Yes, John, we all know that. Don't worry. They are for all of us. Plus, there is more. She has a recipe for a new drink I think you are going to really like. I just had a sip of it, and it may remind you of something you really enjoy at Christmas."

Mr. McGillicuddy stared at her in disbelief. "What, you mean we are celebrating Christmas in the middle of this July heat?"

"You'll see. Come on."

"I know what it is." Remington looked at his grandma and winked.

"Don't say anything else. Let your grandpa find out for himself. So hurry up and come downstairs. Maria is waiting for us. She wants to surprise you."

"Okay, Grandma, we will be right down. We were almost finished."

Mrs. McGillicuddy turned and walked out the door.

Remington stood on his tiptoes and motioned for his grandfather to bend over. He whispered in his ear, "The bulbs really do speak Bulbese. I've actually heard them two different times speaking among themselves. I don't think they knew I heard, but it's like a chattering sound. I will tell you more later."

"What's wrong, dear? Do you feel all right? You look pale."

"I should look pale," grumbled Mr. McGillicuddy. "That stuff was terrible."

"Oh, John, it wasn't that bad. In fact, it was kind of interesting. Maria told me that particular *horchata* was made with earth almond or tiger nut."

"Well, as far as I am concerned, the tigers should drink the stuff, not humans."

Mrs. McGillicuddy laughed.

"And you know, Jane, I like Maria very much. I am glad Richard and Lisa did what they did for her, and I am glad she is Remington's nanny, but I don't have to like that drink. It was awful."

"Well, you might be right. It did have a strange taste to it, although Remington said Spaniards love it and drink it year round. You heard him say it took him a long time to like it."

"Well, I can tell you this. I won't ever have enough time to like that milky stuff."

"You mean my eggnog will still be number one on your list?"

"Even though that apple cinnamon recipe of yours makes me sleepy, my dear, I shall always love your eggnog."

13

Summer Vacation Filled with Danger

For the first week of their second visit to Spain in less than a year, Mr. and Mrs. McGillicuddy, Remington, and his folks visited many places in Madrid and the surrounding areas that they were unable to see during their Christmas time trip. They experienced the fun of returning to Madrid's most famous park, *El Retiro*, where they enjoyed many activities that weren't available to them during the cold weather of December. Paddleboat rides, special nighttime music festivals, and lots of walking and running through the hidden areas of the park made those two days very special.

Plus, there were four days of side trips to small towns near Madrid, where visits to famous cities like Toledo and Segovia allowed them a chance to experience different lifestyles in Spain. They saw some very famous castles and aqueducts dating clear back to the first century when the Romans occupied what was later to become the country of Spain. In all, it was a special week, but the really big vacation was about to begin. And none of the

McGillicuddy family could ever have dreamed how exciting and scary it would be.

The first few days of the second week were spent at the jazz festival in Northern Spain. Remington had tried to act like he was really interested. Each night they listened to the music, but sometimes he found it boring and he had even fallen asleep one night. But he had admitted to his grandfather that the last night of the festival was fun. The famous guitar player, B. B. King, had been the star performer, and Remington really enjoyed his music.

He especially liked it when his mom and dad had left their seats high up in the arena and had gone down near the stage to do something called the "jitterbug." They had been so good at it that the people running the jazz festival had asked them to go up on stage and dance while the musicians played. It had been a fantastic time because the thousands and thousands of people in the audience had cheered loudly for them.

But then came the really fun part of the vacation, five days in the picturesque seaside town of *Peñiscola*.

In June, it is not as hot, and the beaches are not as crowded as they are in August, although there are still thousands of people on vacation. The McGillicuddy family was a small part of those beach walkers and sunbathers,

and they had been having a wonderful time. For three days they had enjoyed the beautiful blue Mediterranean Sea, walking the sandy beaches, romping in the rolling waves, and testing their swimming close to shore.

On the next to last day of their vacation, Remington and his dad got up early so they could find a good spot right next to the water. They could have slept a little longer because there were only a few people on the beach this early, and there was plenty of room to do what they had planned to do for the past two days. Most of the early risers were walking along the edge of the beach, the waves rushing over their feet as they strolled in the sand.

The two of them crossed the street in front of the *Hosteria Del Mar* where they were staying and hurried down to a spot close to the water. Remington went right to work in starting to build a huge sandcastle while his dad put clothes and shoes and a couple of beach chairs nearby, so he could save plenty of room for the rest of the family when they got there. In an hour from now, there would already be hundreds of people setting up beach towels, umbrellas, and lounging chairs to get ready for a day in the sun.

The hour quickly went by as Remington worked on his project. More and more people began to arrive and secure their places in the sand. Remington, with the help of his dad, had already made lots of progress on the start of

an impressive castle that when finished would be about six feet long and three feet wide. It had an interior area that was big enough for Remington to stand inside as he continued to work on the fortress he was building around the castle.

Remington lost track of the time because he was so busy and having so much fun. He had only taken one short break of five minutes while working on the sandy piece of art. He was surprised when his dad walked up with a soft drink for him and told him they had been there for two and a half hours.

Remington had only taken that one brief rest during that whole time. He was still working hard, smoothing out the sand on all sides of the castle and making sure the turrets and the walkway around the top were just right. He was nearing the finish, and the job he had done was so impressive that many, many people walking along the beach were changing direction and strolling down near the water so they could see what he had built. It captivated the attention of sunbathers and others who meandered along the shoreline. Some would just stop and stand motionless, chattering away in many different European languages, while they stared at the huge sculpture. It was now nearly three feet high and was large enough that Remington could actually stand inside the walls and walk around on the cool sand, and he could even sit down inside the structure.

"See how popular you have become, Remington?"

The current group of interested beach strollers had stopped and peeked over the side and had waved at him just as he looked up from his sitting position next to one of the corners of the fortress. He was making sure the lookout tower he had built at the corner of one of the walkways on top was just right.

He waved back at the latest circle of visitors and said to his dad, "Do you think I should charge money for these people to visit my castle?"

His dad laughed. "I should have known you would finally think of that. Maybe you could lay out a big towel and put a dish with some euros inside it, and people would think you are the youngest artist working on the beach."

"Really, Daddy. Could I?"

"Oh, Remi. I was only kidding."

"Oh, all right. I thought you really meant it."

Suddenly, a baldheaded man with a potbelly hanging over his swim trunks and a sunburned bare chest leaned down, and in an accent Remington had never heard, said, "I understand English. You do good work on the castle. You get money, no?"

Remington's dad started to say that Remington didn't get money, but he didn't have a chance. The man leaned down and handed Remington a ten Euro bill.

"For me?" squealed Remington.

"Yes, for you, my little friend," and then the man and four other people in the group all applauded and smiled.

They turned to walk away, and Remington's dad said, "Oh, you can't do that. He didn't expect that money."

"No, *mein herr*," one of the women said. "My husband knows. But he says the boy deserves the euros." And before anything else was said, the five of them walked away.

A moment later, Remington yelled to them, "Thank you and my dad said—" and then Remington stopped and looked up at his father. "How did you say that word, Daddy?"

"*Danke schoen*," his dad yelled to the group. Three of them turned around and waved back and shouted, "*Bitte schoen.*"

"That's 'thank you' in German. I was pretty sure they were from Germany when I heard the man's accent. You know, I told you thousands of Germans come to Peñiscola every summer for their vacations.

"And by the way, if you will turn around and look behind you—" he reached down and put his hands on Remington's shoulders—"you will see some other people on vacation who are not from Germany."

Then he turned Remington around so he could see his mom and grandparents. They had crossed the street in front of the hotel and were walking down the wooden

walk that stretched from the sidewalk almost all the way through the sand to near the edge of the water.

"Oh, I can't wait to tell them I got paid to make a castle." He took off running and waving his arms wildly in the air.

"What are you so excited about? I saw you down at the water with your dad. Is something wrong?"

"No, Grandpa. Nothing is wrong. Everything is great. I can't wait to show all of you the castle I have built. It is *huge*. Wait till you see it."

"Well, then let's hurry because I have a surprise for you."

"Really? What is it, Mom?"

"Maybe I should wait until we see the castle."

"Well, that's okay if you want. I mean all we have to do is walk between all these sunbathers in the sand, and we will be there in a minute. In fact, look! You can see the castle from here. See, Dad is waving, and he's standing next to it."

His grandmother stopped abruptly, her hand shading her eyes. "Oh, my gosh, Remington. How did you do that? It looks like it's higher than your dad's knees. How did you build it so quickly?"

"It wasn't quick. Dad and I sneaked out of the room at seven o'clock. You guys are the sleepy heads. It's nearly eleven. I've had lots of time to work on it.

"Duh-dah! Here it is," said Remington, and he stretched his arms out to both sides with the palms of his hands facing upward. "What do you think?"

His mom had a wide smile on her face. "It is fantastic, Remington. You did a great job. My gosh, honey, did you help him with this?"

"I helped him smooth up the sides, but that is all. It was his whole idea, the walkway around the top, the turrets, everything."

"Thanks, Dad, but it was nice having you here cheering me on."

"Well, I bet someone else wants to cheer you on."

"Who is that?"

Remington's mom reached into her beach bag. She moved the towels and suntan lotion out of the way and pulled out the blue bulb. "After what happened to your grandfather at the castle yesterday and how this silly bulb apparently had something to do in finding him, I am ready to admit that we have a magical little guy here, who we probably should keep quiet about. Otherwise, people will believe we are all crazy."

Everybody started laughing. Remington stood looking at the four of them, and he started to get angry that they were making fun of Bobby, but then he realized his mom was right. How could anyone ever believe all the sensational and daring things his magical bulb had done?

He smiled and also laughed. "I think you're right. Let's keep the news to ourselves, but thanks for bringing him here. I didn't want to lose him by mistake when I left this morning, so I thought it would be safer to keep him in the room."

"Well, why don't we put him in a special place in your castle?" She bent over and placed the blue bulb right on top of one of the four towers that were on each corner. "See, he kind of looks like a king sitting up there."

"Oh, Mom. You are the greatest, and thanks for finally believing in Bobby." Remington jumped into his mother's arms, knocked the beach bag out of her hands, and gave her a big hug and kiss.

"Listen," Remington's dad said. "Why don't we move back a few feet from the castle. I saved this area right here for us. I scattered our shoes and towels in the sand so no one will take this space."

"Well, I just ordered three more chairs from the hotel's beach booth," Remington's mom added, "and in fact, I see the guy bringing them right now." She pointed at a beach worker who was dragging the heavy chairs through the sand. "So, let's get comfortable and enjoy Remington's castle."

Remington played with Bobby and walked him around the top of the castle. He talked to the bulb, and when everyone was busy setting up the chairs and getting comfortable, Bobby squeaked, "I looove you."

"Beep, b-e-e-e-e-e-e-e-e-e-e-p, b-e-e-e-p too, Bobby. I tell you what, let's go take a quick swim together. I will put you in the pocket of my swimming trunks so you don't get too wet. The cool water will feel good. Let's do it while my folks are getting the chairs set up and fixing the food for lunch."

Remington grabbed the bulb, stuffed it deep into the pocket of his swim trunks, and ran into the water.

At that moment, his dad looked up and shouted, "You be careful and don't go too far."

Remington dashed through the water and ran into an incoming wave that splashed water all over his swimsuit and part of his chest. He looked back over his shoulder and yelled, "I'm only going to right here, Daddy. Everything is fine."

But little did Remington know that by the time the sun was setting much later in the day, nothing would be fine and there would only be sadness.

"Remington. Remington! Come back in closer. That's far enough."

Remington saw his mom waving her arms and motioning for him to come back in toward shore.

Remington had been in and out of the water for all day, and he was getting tired. He ducked under a wave and let

the power of the current push him along the sandy bottom until he came to a stop. Then, he sat up and brushed salty water off his face before he stood up in the knee-deep water. Just as he did, a giant wave crushed into his back, and he was knocked down. He lay in the water for a few seconds and then jumped up quickly when he heard his dad's voice. "I'm okay," he yelled, and he waved at his family, who were sitting side by side in their beach chairs.

He let the water swirl across his feet as it rushed back into the sea. He then walked a few feet and stepped onto the beach. He took four or five more steps before he dropped down on his knees into the hot sand in front of his castle.

"Time to put you back on top of the turret so people walking by can see our hero," Remington said as he started to reach into his pocket. But just as he did, he felt two hands on his shoulders. He turned his head and looked up into the smiling face of his grandfather. "Oh, my gosh! You scared me, Grandpa."

"Well, I meant to," Mr. McGillicuddy said and grinned some more. "I'm thinking about rolling you around in this sand so you will have to go back out in the water and wash off. Then, I could come with you. Did you have a good time out there? It looked like you were swimming pretty good."

"We had a great time, Grandpa. At least, I think Bobby did."

"You took the bulb out into the water when you went swimming?" his mother said as she and Mrs. McGillicuddy walked up to join them.

"It's okay, Mom. He's deep in the pocket of my trunks."

"Well, I just noticed it wasn't sitting on the top of the castle. I was afraid somebody might have picked it up when they were walking by, and we weren't paying attention."

Remington started to reach into his pocket again. "No, he's right here," but before he got his hand completely into the pocket, he felt another pair of hands on his shoulders.

"What is this?" he squealed. "Everybody is scaring me by walking up behind me and grabbing my shoulders. Grandpa did it a minute ago and now you, Dad. What's going on?"

"Hey, I'm just hungry and ready to take all of you to that neat little restaurant we saw yesterday. Those sandwiches your mom made weren't enough to satisfy me."

"Dad, is that the one you are talking about, the one over there?" Remington pointed across a tiny cove at the boat dock. It sat at the bottom of a rocky slope that led up to the castle, which overlooked the long strip of hotels and motels along the miles and miles of sandy beach.

"That's the one I'm thinking about."

"Yippee!" Remington stood up and grabbed his hand just as his dad said, "Let's go, everybody. We will take a walk up to the main avenue and then we will wander down the long walkway and look at all of the beach sculptures in the sand. When we are finished we can come back down to the water and it will be only a short walk around this little bay and we will be right there at the restaurant."

Remington started to giggle and he looked up at his grandfather. "Well, let's get going because by the time we get that walk finished I will be starving, and of course we already know Granddaddy is always hungry."

Everyone laughed as they gathered up their beach bags and towels. Ten minutes later they began their roundabout stroll that would eventually take them to the restaurant that was only a few hundred yards away. As they trekked through the sand, Remington and his dad tried to kick the soccer ball along the sandy beach, but time after time ended up kicking it into the water where one of them would have to dash into the sea and retrieve it.

"I can only hope we can reach the wide sidewalk soon so there is no place to kick that ball," Mrs. McGillicuddy said. "Otherwise, we will never have enough time to go to the restaurant as bad as you two are at controlling that soccer ball."

"You're right, Grandma. We aren't very good, but we are having fun."

In fact, Remington was having such a fantastic time running and playing along the beach that he never once thought about his special little friend. Later in the evening when they reached the restaurant and enjoyed a dinner filled with *tapas, paella,* and some great *tartas con fresas,* he still didn't think about his best friend who had taught him so much the past few months.

In fact, it wasn't until the five happy members of the McGillicuddy family finished their relaxing three-hour dinner and had strolled along the sandy beach for another hour that Remington discovered the terrible and frightening news.

14

Lost at Sea

"**C**an I go first?" Remington asked his parents.

"Do you think it is okay, Richard?"

"Of course. It's only a couple a hundred feet, and we can certainly see him. That's what is nice about it being nine-thirty and still nearly an hour of daylight left."

"All right, go ahead," she said.

He stepped onto the wooden planked walkway. "Can I run all the way to the street? I'll wait for you."

"Just be careful," said his dad. "Don't get your feet caught between the slats in the boardwalk."

Remington dashed away, and his parents and grandparents watched. Less than a minute later, they saw him stop and wave to them as he stood at the end of the walkway near the sidewalk. They waved back, and then the four of them began slowly walking up the sloping plank toward the hotel.

The two-lane avenue between the beach and the hotels was filled with automobiles moving slowly, almost bumper-to-bumper, in both directions. Parents and their

children walked leisurely side by side on a tiled sidewalk that was nearly as wide as one of the street lanes. Couples stopped to stare out toward the sea. An occasional jogger trotted by enjoying some late-evening exercise. Youngsters on skateboards and roller skates were also part of the scene, causing a few strollers to stare or yell at them as they dangerously ducked in and out among the crowd. The scene was similar to slow flowing water in a creek or river—hundreds of people talking, laughing, and enjoying themselves on the boulevard that stretched for miles and miles alongside the beaches of Peñiscola.

Therefore, it was easy to understand why the never-ending noise of talking, laughter, and the occasional honking of horns from frustrated drivers drowned out the initial cries of the little boy standing next to the shower stall at the end of the walkway.

However, when that same little boy continued to scream even louder and louder, a couple standing at a nearby sidewalk bench heard him. When they turned to look, they saw the boy run down the wooden walkway and suddenly trip and fall face down into the sand. They watched for a moment, and when he didn't appear to move, they hurried down the walkway. The man jumped into the sand and dropped to his knees to take a look at the little boy.

Remington's parents and grandparents were laughing and telling stories. Twice they stopped, and all four

of them turned around to look back out at the sea, now beginning to be covered with strips of moonlight, which highlighted the waves rushing into the shore. Mr. McGillicuddy was leading the way up the walkway and in front of the other three. He was the first who heard the noise.

"Oh, no! That sounds like Remington's voice. He's screaming. Something must be wrong."

The others turned around, and then in the distance, they all saw a man down on his knees. He, and a woman standing next to him, was bending over a boy, and there was no doubt it was Remington.

"Oh, my God!" Remington's dad jumped into the sand, raced around Mr. McGillicuddy, and leaped back onto the walkway. He ran as fast as he could.

"What's happening, what is wrong?" yelled Remington's dad. When the man and woman kneeling in the sand didn't answer, he switched to Spanish.

"¿Que es el problema?" He shouted even louder. He was almost there, and he could see Remington pounding his fists into the sand.

"No, lo se, señor. Se parece bien, pero esta gritando."

Remington's dad ran the last few feet through the sand and dropped down on his knees. "Muchisimas gracias con su ayuda, señor."

"No hay de que."

"Remington, it's Daddy. What's wrong, buddy?"

Suddenly, Remington rolled on to his back and stared up at his father and a man and woman he didn't know. "He's gone. Bobby is gone." Remington began crying and yelling. "I can't find him. I think he is in the water. I think I lost him."

"Is he all right?" Remington's mom came trudging through the sand. In the distance behind her, Mr. and Mrs. McGillicuddy were hurrying along the walkway as fast as they could.

"*Señor, ¿necesita una ambulancia?*"

Remington's dad looked up and saw a policeman hurrying toward the group.

"*Esta bien. Ha perdido algo. Esta bien. Gracias a ustedes.*"

"What's happened, Richard? Is he okay? What are you telling that policeman?"

Remington continued to lie on his back, but the screaming had stopped. He was sobbing, and both of his arms were wrapped tightly around his chest.

She reached down to hug her son and to wipe away some tears. "The policeman. What does he want?"

"I told him we don't need an ambulance. Remington is okay, or at least, he's not hurt. See, the policeman is getting everyone to move back."

"Well, what happened?"

"I didn't want to tell them Remington was throwing a fit because he lost a Christmas tree light bulb."

"What? Oh, Remi. You lost your bulb."

Remington started crying again, and he began screaming once more. People walking away stopped for a moment and turned to look again.

"What's wrong with him, Lisa?"

When Remington saw his granddad approaching, he suddenly pulled loose from the arms of his mom. He jumped to his feet and ran to his grandfather. He hugged him around his waist. "You know how special he was, Granddaddy. I've lost him. Bobby is lost."

"Your blue bulb? Are you sure?"

Tears streamed down his face. "Yes. I've looked in all of the pockets of my swim trunks. I thought he was in there. That's where I put him, and I was sure he was in there when I got out of the water. Oh, Grandpa, he's lost. He must have fallen out of my trunks while I was in the water. But I don't know how because I snapped that pocket shut. At least, I thought I did. I've got to go find him. I've got to look on the beach. Will you come with me?"

Remington turned and looked at all four faces staring at him. "We are family. You've got to help me." And he turned and raced through the sand.

His mother moved to grab him, just missing. "Remington. Wait! It's almost dark."

Richard put his arms around her shoulders. "Oh, let him go. Come on. Let's all go. At least we can look along the shore until there is no light. There's no chance, but at least let's do it for Remington's sake."

15
The Search

"It's going to be completely dark in five more minutes, Remi. We are lucky the moon is three-quarters full, or we couldn't see anything. At least we have a little bit of light left."

"I know, Granddad, but it won't make any difference." The tears continued to roll down his face. "It will never be the same again. We will never find him. I miss him so much."

Remington saw his dad walking back out of the water. "We can't find anything, Remington. Mom and Grandma and I have each walked along the beach for twenty or thirty yards on each side of your castle. It just isn't possible to find him, buddy."

Remington started crying even louder. He shouted, "I am so dumb. Why did I take him in the water? It wasn't like I thought he could swim."

"It will be okay, sweetheart. I'm feeling bad about this. If I hadn't picked it up and brought it to you, it would still be in the hotel room. I just thought you would want

him at the beach. But, we will just have to find another blue bulb for you."

"Oh, Mom. Get real. We will never find another bulb like him. He was magical. You know he was. You finally had to admit it. But it wasn't your fault, Mom. It was mine. I just wanted to be with dad and make a castle and I didn't want to bring Bobby. But, I was glad when you did and I felt guilty I hadn't brought him to the beach. And now," Remington started sobbing again, "he is gone forever."

Mr. McGillicuddy was standing next to both of them, and he reached down and picked up his grandson. He started to say something but Remington threw his arms around his neck and whispered into his ear, "Oh, Grandpa, you knew before anybody how great he was, didn't you?"

Mr. McGillicuddy started to answer, but suddenly saw a flashlight beam sweeping through the sand. He peered over the brightness of the light and saw a man walking toward them. "Richard, that man has a flashlight."

Remington's dad recognized the man when a moonbeam fell across his face. "It's that same policeman who was up at the sidewalk."

"Oh, Daddy, ask him if we can borrow his flashlight. Maybe he can help us."

16
Blue Buried Treasure

He didn't know how many hours he had been lying there. But he thought for at least the last couple of hours he had heard voices. At least he thought it had been a couple of hours. He had always been good at keeping time but mostly by days. In the past, he remembered Remington talking about hours and minutes, but it had always been difficult for him to try and figure out short periods of time.

However, one thing was for certain. Even though it was cooler since the sun had finally set, the sand still felt warm to him. He had been soaked and covered with water when he had flown nose first into the white, gritty stuff. He had nearly been buried. It had been extremely hot at the time, and he had chuckled and wondered if food felt like this when it was inside one of those things humans called ovens.

But the longer he had been stuck in the sand, the longer he had realized there was nothing funny about any of this. He was completely exhausted, and he knew he was very lucky to be alive.

Now, he was feeling a little better because he had managed to twist himself back and forth in the sand. He had freed himself enough to roll into an upright position, and he could see the sky above.

He could see streaks of what people called moonlight. He remembered two years ago at Christmas when Remington had explained to him one night in his bedroom what the moon was. He always thought it must be like a big nighttime flashlight for humans.

He looked up and saw the walls surrounding him. If only he had enough strength to make a noise, maybe someone nearby would find him. *"Oh, yeah, like someone here in Spain is going to understand a bulb squeaking. I wish Remington had taught me how to say 'help.'"*

Then he laughed. *"Listen to me talking to myself. No one cares. I guess even Remington doesn't care. He's forgotten me. I wonder if he even knows I'm gone. I wonder if he will ever know what happened."* As he pondered that thought, he suddenly shivered and felt a tingle race through his filaments.

During all of the danger of the past few hours, he had not taken time even once to think of his own family. The thought was terrible. Would they ever know what happened to him?

The entire day he had enjoyed hearing Remington screaming and laughing and having fun running through the water and diving into the waves. Tucked inside the

pocket of the swim trunks, Bobby could feel the coolness of the water, especially when one of those big waves would splash up against Remington. It was a little scary when the waves knocked Remington down because he would end up sitting on the sandy bottom of the sea, and Bobby would feel the water swirling around the pocket. He was sure he was safe, but whenever the water would rush across Remington, Bobby would get that momentary feeling of being trapped.

He had really been nervous at first, but Remington had told him to "Chill out. You will be safe, little buddy." Remington explained to him that the pocket was "waterproof." The word meant that water would not get inside the pocket even though the trunks were wet.

He had been happy that Remington was having fun, but it sure seemed like he had been in the water a long time. No matter what Remington said about the pocket being waterproofed, Bobby still felt cold and damp. And he was tired of being jostled around. Each time Remington was knocked down, Bobby was crunched against the side of his body. It reminded him of that crunching sound he had heard two years ago when the tornado had struck the McGillicuddy's house and Bobby's dad and cousin, Whitening, had accidentally been stepped on in the closet.

He had been thinking about that terrible moment when something strange happened. He felt himself slide

backward, and he began to bounce around inside the pocket. He realized Remington was running in the water.

As he was jostled back and forth, he was surprised when he looked up and actually saw the sky. It took only a moment before he realized what was happening. He was about to fall out of the pocket, and the reason was the flap that kept it closed had become unbuttoned. He was in danger.

He continued to slip and slide, and he barely managed to stay inside the pocket. He tried to roll himself deeper into it, but each step Remington took caused Bobby to bounce back near the pocket's edge. This was a disaster about to happen. And then it did. A giant wave from behind had pounded Remington face forward into the water. As Remington hit the shallow sandy bottom, Bobby felt the water rush over him.

A few moments later, he couldn't believe it. He was still inside the pocket. He was safe for the moment, but just barely. He could see Remington's head face down in the wet sand. Bobby wondered if he was hurt, but Remington quickly jumped up and started laughing. He yelled to someone that he was "okay."

But Bobby was far from okay. When Remington stood up, Bobby had felt himself slipping, and he dropped out of the pocket. He fell into very shallow water that was no more than two or three inches deep. *This was at least good*, he thought. *Since the water isn't deep, I might*

have a chance to roll forward onto the beach. He knew he would have to move quickly, and he started to say his magical word *puhrumba* but didn't have a chance. Those tiny trickles of water around him suddenly became a huge wave, and he was engulfed by it. He had no time to twist and roll toward the dry sand. He felt the undertow of the sea sucking him away from the beach and into deep water, and he knew his life was probably over.

At that moment, as he continued to remember what had happened to him in the past few hours, Bobby thought back to a conversation with his dad just about a week before he had left on this trip with Remington. *"You know you have told us many times how you have always heard Mr. McGillicuddy say he wished he was more 'lucky.' Well, I don't have to wish, Bobby. I know I am lucky."* Then his dad had explained how fortunate he knew he was to have survived the accident in the closet two years ago, and how lucky he was that he and the other bulbs had kept him safe while hiding him from the McGillicuddys. And he had told Bobby he certainly knew he was lucky to be able to live on the strand with his family, even though he had a chip in his head.

It was amazing, Bobby thought, *that something like this would flash through your mind as you were whirling through the water.* The further he was pushed from shore, the more he bounced into seashells and small rocks lying on the bottom. In a matter of a few seconds

he knew his life was over and there was no hope. But he was wrong. He was about to learn, as his father had, what being lucky was all about.

The force of the water was so strong that he was completely out of control. He was thrown through the waves with such power that he bounced and skipped off the bottom of the sea, crashing into more small rocks. For the briefest moment, as he pummeled forward, he thought how lucky he was he had not been smashed into pieces. And then he crashed into something different. He had no idea what it was, but he could tell it was standing in the water, and it was much softer than the things he had been hitting and bouncing off of.

The moment he struck it, a huge wave on the surface forced a change of direction. The current on the sea floor reversed, and as the water moved toward shore, he thought he heard the sound of a human voice.

The force of the giant wave propelled him upward and out of the water. Sailing above the surface, he caught a glimpse of a bald-headed man with a big belly standing and looking toward the shore.

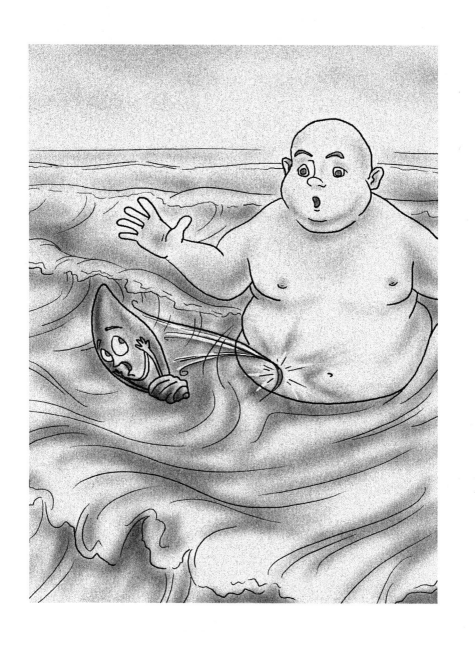

In that instant, he realized how lucky he had been. If he had not smashed into the man's leg, the power of the current would have pushed him further out to sea. He would have had no chance to survive. Now, maybe there was hope. As he fell back into the water, he skipped across the top of the surface. He got another lucky break when another set of large waves pushed him forward even faster. The next thing he knew, he was slamming nose-first into wet sand. He hit the beach so hard that his whole body immediately ached, but once again, he had been lucky.

It took a few minutes to finally twist and wiggle himself loose from the sand. When he had flipped himself up onto his pod, he saw he was actually clear from the water and lying on the edge of the wet beach. As he rotated so he could see where he was, he nearly jumped into the air. He was lying next to an old dead crab that was halfway buried in the sand.

He was safe for the moment, but he knew that at any second, a strong wave could come rushing up onto the beach, and the tide could pull him out into the sea again. He had to completely escape from the water. He turned away from that ugly-looking crab, and when he did, he saw something in the opposite direction that gave him a flicker of hope.

Was he seeing things? He wasn't sure, so he shook his body from side to side to make sure his vision was

perfect. He again looked into the distance, and then he was certain. At least he thought he was, and to be absolutely sure, he shook one more time. Now he knew he was right. There they were, all five of them, holding their shoes in their hands, and walking through the shallow water as it splashed over their feet.

"*Oh, my gosh! I'm going to be okay if I can just get to Remington. I bet he doesn't even know he's lost me. What a surprise when I fly up to him.*" Then he looked at them again walking together but they were much further down the beach. He was afraid it was too far for him to fly in his condition, but he had to try. He shouted his powerful words, "*Puhrumba! Puhrumba! Puhrumba!*"

He waited for the first shiver that always raced through his body before he lifted off the ground. But this time, there was no weird, shaking feeling. There wasn't even a twitch in his body. There wasn't any hope. Remington would never know what happened to him, and Bobby wondered if Remington would even care.

"*What's wrong with me? I've got to stop feeling sorry for myself and get out of here.*" He shouted the words three more times, and when nothing happened, he shouted another three times. Now he became panicky. *What am I going to do?*

It was at that moment he saw them. A group of young children who looked like they were Remington's age were walking toward where he was lying. They were busily

picking up seashells, and now they were just a few yards away. *"What if they see me and want to take me with them? I've got to get out of here, now."*

His filaments began to shake. Had he finally run out of luck? A split second later, he got the answer.

He had not run out of luck.

Another wave, larger than any of the others he had seen all day, cascaded toward the beach; and as the water rushed over him, he was driven off of the wet edge of the beach and tossed completely away from the water, landing in a clump of hot, gritty, white sand. He lay there for a moment, not sure of actually what had happened but knowing he had been very, very lucky. He had been swept away from the edge of the water and appeared safe for the moment even if he was partially covered by the hot sand.

Now he had hope. If he could get lucky one more time and somehow reach the sandcastle, he would be safe from people stepping on him or picking him up and walking away with him.

He knew he needed some rest in order to regain some of his power, and he had waited a few minutes before he started wiggling. He managed to rise up into a sitting position. But he was there for only a few seconds before he had to duck back down in the sand when two big feet clomped past him. He waited to see if there was anyone else walking by, and when he didn't hear anything, he once

more pulled himself up into a sitting position. But his timing was bad, and he again had to duck down when he saw a woman walking toward where he was sitting. This time, though, he wasn't quite as fortunate. One of her beach sandals brushed up against him, and when it did, he was squashed even deeper into the sand.

But then he realized he had been lucky again. *I could have been smashed into tiny pieces*, he thought. *Well, one thing is certain. I better get out of here, or I am going to get hurt. I hope I haven't used up all of my luck. I'm going to scream twice as many times as before.*

And then in a voice like the sound of a hundred sizzling fireworks he shouted, "*Puhrumba! Puhrumba! Puhrumba! Puhrumba! Puhrumba! Puhrumba!*"

"*Puhrumba! Puhrumba! Puhrumba! Puhrumba! Puhrumba! Puhrumba!*" The magical cry was so loud and so high pitched, several dogs on the beach began howling. The noise was at such a level that only the dogs heard it. Sunbathers, swimmers, and people strolling on the beach looked in every direction to try and see what the barking and whining was all about.

The sand flew into the air, twisting and spinning, and looking very much like a small tornado. The children he had just seen picking up seashells turned and stared at the block of sand whirling in the air. It was like a huge, white funnel, and people nearby shielded their eyes as sand whirled fifteen to twenty feet above the ground.

Swimmers jumped out of the water to see what happened, and families playing in the waves near shore all turned and stared in amazement. Three teenagers, two boys and a girl, were racing toward the flying sand hoping to get a closer look. Within a few yards in either direction, people were pointing and staring and chattering in a number of different languages.

As for Bobby, he continued to be lucky. He was certain no one could see him because of the swirling sand. He kept spinning as hard as he could, and as he did, the funnel moved closer and closer to the sandcastle that was now only a few feet away. But he knew he had to hurry. Time was running out because his frightening experience in the water had sapped nearly all of the strength from his body.

He knew he no longer had any kind of a chance to reach Remington and his family. He had to get inside that sandcastle, and he had to hurry. Suddenly, he began to lose the power he had produced when he had escaped the sand trap. He could feel it leaving his body, and the blanket of white and brown sprinkles of sand that had protected him from being seen started to loosen and fall downward to the beach.

He nearly panicked because he was afraid he was going to drop right back down into the sand. However, he was able to tilt his head, and when he looked down, he realized

he still had a little bit of luck left. There he was staring directly into Remington's sandcastle and fortress.

All he had to do was dive straight down, and he would be safe; but he had to hurry because the sand that shielded him had almost completely disappeared, and someone could easily see him. That was the last thing he needed to happen. He just wanted to get inside that sand sculpture and hope that Remington and his family would find him. They were leaving to return to Madrid the next day, and he could only hope they would come back by the sandcastle before they returned to their hotel across the street.

He had survived because he had been lucky. He had bounced off seashells and hard rocks. He had been washed ashore by powerful waves. He had been stepped on by a woman's sandal and nearly crushed. And, when he had dove into the open area of the castle, he had crashed off the wall of the fortress. He was hurt, and he was sore and totally exhausted from his scary adventure. But he was certain he was safe, although he knew it would take some work to get free from the sand. He was buried all the way to the end of his pod.

He looked back up to the sky. He saw streaks of orange among the clouds. It would soon be dark. Thinking back to what had happened to him over the past three hours had taken away even more of his strength. He just wanted to lay there and hope Remington would return.

17
The Search Continues

The policeman had been very helpful. Remington's dad walked with him as he moved the flashlight beam up and down the beach. They had spoken Spanish, and when they discovered that Remington's dad knew the policeman's brother, who happened to work as a guard at the US Embassy in Madrid, the policeman radioed for more help.

When two more policemen arrived, Remington and his grandfather went with one of them, and his mom and grandmother searched with the third one. But after thirty minutes, there was no luck; and finally, everyone met near the little sandcastle and admitted there was no hope. Now Remington's dad and mom were thanking the policemen one more time before they left, and Remington sat near the water's edge looking out at the sea and wiping tears from his eyes.

Mr. McGillicuddy had his arms around the waist of his wife, and he leaned down and said, "I don't know when I have felt worse. That bulb meant everything to

Remington, and, Jane, you have to admit, it did have some magical qualities. We were part of seeing some true miracles from that little guy."

"John, that sounds so stupid to say something like that, but I have to agree with you. It was almost like having an extraterrestrial creature with us at times."

Mr. McGillicuddy chuckled and said, "I guess you're right. I had never thought about it like that."

The policemen were trudging up through the sand, and they turned to wave one more time. Remington's mom and dad waved back, and then they walked over to their son. Right behind them came Mrs. McGillicuddy, and the three hugged each other and stood back and watched Remington continue to cry. "Best to let him get it out of his system," said his dad, and both women nodded their heads in agreement.

Mr. McGillicuddy stood by himself a few feet away. He was wiping tears from his eyes with the back of his hand. When he was finished, he walked away from where the water had been lapping up close to his feet.

He looked back toward the area where Richard and the policeman had been standing just a few minutes earlier. For just a second, he thought he saw something. A sliver of moonlight had flashed across some kind of an object. He walked off the wet part of the beach and stomped into the deeper sand. As he got closer, he realized he had seen something. He took a few more steps toward it,

and when he leaned down to look, he saw one of the three flashlights that had been used by the policemen.

He quickly looked toward the street and boulevard, but they had disappeared. No chance to give them back the flashlight right now, so he picked it up, and as the tears moistened in his eyes again, he slowly walked along the beach. He turned on the flashlight and swept its shaft of light across the thick mounds of sand.

He saw the sandcastle just a few feet away, and when he did, he thought of how proud Remington had been when he built it and how happy he had been when he had put the blue bulb near one of the turrets of the fortress. It made him sad, and he started to sob once more. "I just can't help myself." He looked toward the water and saw his wife, son, and daughter-in-law all trying to comfort Remington.

A couple of minutes later, after slowly moving along the beach, pointing the light directly down into the sand, he decided it was time to give up. He had seen nothing that looked like a bulb. He was about ten yards past the sandcastle, and he turned and gazed back at his family. He started walking toward them. It was then he heard his wife holler, "Where did you get that flashlight?"

He wasn't sure what she said, and he started to shout back to her but decided that with the sound of the waves crashing into the beach, she probably wouldn't hear anyway. He increased his pace, but after only a few steps his

right knee struck the edge of a lifeguard boat sitting in the sand. He stumbled, and he quickly reached down with his right hand to keep from falling to the ground. When he did, his left hand, which was holding the flashlight, moved forward, and the brightness of the beam swept across the middle of the sandcastle. Despite his attempt to balance himself, he fell face first into the sand.

He lay there for a few seconds, and then he heard voices yelling his name. His nose hurt just a little, but at that moment, he wouldn't have cared if he had broken it. It would have been worth it because of what he had seen.

The image flashed before him. As he had fallen, the beam revealed a tiny object sitting up against the wall in the corner of the fortress. He was sure of it. He leaped back up and on to his feet. He didn't bother to wipe the sand off his trousers. He picked up the flashlight, which he had dropped when he had fallen down, and he pointed the beam inside the sand sculpture. A big grin splashed across his face, and he saw his family running toward him. They were shouting, "Are you all right? Did you hurt yourself?"

But he paid no attention. He just kept grinning, and then he screamed at the top of his lungs, "I found him. I found Bobby."

His family rushed up to him, and they saw tears rolling down his cheeks. "What is it?" Mrs. McGillicuddy gasped.

He just pointed to the inside of the castle. They looked and then Remington screamed with delight, "It's him! Oh, Grandpa. It is Bobby. You found him." Remington reached down and grabbed the bulb. He began to cry with delight, and when he stood up he could see there wasn't a dry eye among any of them.

As the four adults stood there and watched the little boy who was so special and precious to all of them, they each knew they had learned a special lesson during this vacation trip: don't ever take anything for granted.

"I am sorry I lost you, Bobby. But I'm even sorrier it took me so long to realize it. I will never do anything with you again without checking on you all of the time."

Cuddled in the hand of Remington, Bobby looked up and smiled. *Oh, what a story I have to tell my family.*

18

Vacation over, and the Truth Comes Out

During the night and early morning hours, the bedroom was pitch-black dark. In the daytime, a few tiny rays of light would manage to sneak through the window shutters, which actually were metal doors that slid up and down and were very common in apartment buildings throughout Madrid. As another summer day was ending and evening settled in on *Calle Fomento*, the last snippets of sunshine had disappeared about thirty minutes ago. Three blocks away at the church that was nearest the Royal Palace, the eleventh chime on the huge clock in the steeple rang, and then there was silence.

The strand of Christmas tree lights on the windowsill was also filled with silence. When Bobby was away, it always seemed like the bulbs didn't talk as much as when he was there. And since he had been gone so many days, there wasn't much left to talk about, anyway.

"Isn't it amazing?" Glaring asked as she looked at her sister across the empty pod to her right.

"What's amazing?"

"You know, for all those years when we spent nearly eleven months in the closet at the McGillicuddy's house, I never was able to count the days, or even really cared."

Bobby's mom started to say something to her sister, but Glaring continued, "And it really didn't matter to me because it was such a long time it just seemed like it would never end. Only Bobby's countdown as we got closer to Thanksgiving Day made it easier. But after that terrible tornado two years ago when we were in that box in the living room, for weeks and weeks, when the house was being repaired, I asked Bobby to help me learn how to count days."

"Glaring, what are you talking about? Is there something you are trying to say?"

"Well, give me time," she snapped back at her sister. "What I am trying to say is that I have been counting the days since he left with Remington. If I have not made a mistake, and if I understood Bobby correctly, this should have been the day they were supposed to return from vacation."

"You mean I get to see my son tonight. Oh, Glaring, I'm sorry I sounded so ugly a moment ago." She leaned as far as she could to her left, and Glaring did the same to her right, and across that empty pod where Bobby lived they clinked sides.

"I knew you'd be surprised," said Glaring. "However, it looks like I'm wrong. It's now completely dark again, and there is certainly no one in the house. I was hoping I could surprise you with this news, but I must have counted wrong."

"Well, don't give up hope. You know how it is in Spain. Some people are just now sitting down to eat dinner in this country. I bet you're right, Glaring. At least, I hope you are. Let's keep our filaments crossed that they get home tonight. I know Bobby will have lots of stories to tell us."

Two hours later, the door of Remington's bedroom flew open, and he stepped into the room and flicked on the light switch. He ran across the room to the windowsill.

"There's your family. You're back home, Bobby." He took the blue bulb out of his hand and quickly screwed it into the empty socket. He started to say something else, but his mother walked into the room.

"Good, I see you've put your bulb buddy to bed. Now, you get a quick shower because you're filthy after tromping around through those three parks we visited today."

"I'm not really that dirty, Mom. Can't I take a shower in the morning?"

"Remington, please. Just look at you. You look like you've been rolling around in the dirt. Don't argue with me. Get in the shower and then get into bed. All of us are exhausted, but we can sleep late tomorrow."

"Okay, that's good news. I'm tired of getting up early and going to see castles and museums, and all that other stuff."

"So you didn't enjoy our trip?"

"I didn't mean that, Mom. You know, I'm just tired of getting up early every morning."

"Well, you got to sleep late every morning in Vitoria because we stayed up late every night at the jazz festival."

"Yeah, but that was just three days."

"Oh, you poor little soul. What a tough vacation you had." She laughed and hugged her son. "One thing's for certain, between what happened to your grandpa and that blue bulb of yours, I don't think we will ever forget *Peñiscola* and the end of our trip."

Remington smiled as he looked up at his mom. "You know now, don't you, Mom, that he really is incredible and magical too."

"Yes, I know I am crazy to believe all of those things, but I do. I suppose I won't question anything about your blue bulb ever again. I'm glad Bobby was found and he wasn't lost in the Mediterranean Sea. And for certain we know Grandpa is happy that Bobby helped us find him so he didn't spend the night locked up in the castle. But I do think your grandfather is still a little confused about everything."

Remington looked at her and smiled. "Hey, you know Granddaddy and me. We just like to cause a little excitement. Just like I did last Christmas at *Cortylandia.*"

"Don't even remind me. I still get the shakes when I think about you lost on those dark, downtown streets. Now, for the final time, Remington McGillicuddy, it is one fifteen in the morning. Go take your shower and get in bed."

"Okay. But it will be short. I am tired." His mom kissed him on the forehead and quickly left the room. He went into the bathroom, closed the door, and within moments was in the shower.

Bobby could hear the steady pitter-pat of the water hitting the shower curtain. It made him sleepy, and even though he had been awake for many hours and they had traveled many miles, he knew he was going to have to tell some stories about the trip before he could sleep.

It was as if Aunt Glaring had just read his mind. *"Well, are you going to tell us what happened?"*

Before he could answer, Dazzling shouted from the middle of the strand, *"Oh, you've got to tell us everything. Were there any exciting, mysterious things that happened? We are glad you are back. Please tell us now*

and don't make us wait. It's not fair if you don't tell us the story now."

"Yes, Bobby," urged his brother, Dimmer. "Please tell us what happened."

"Listen, I'm going to tell you about a bunch of things that happened, but I can't get started because Remington will be back in here, and he will be going to sleep. Can't you wait until in the morning when he is having breakfast?"

"No, I don't think that's acceptable," bellowed Uncle Flicker at the opposite end of the windowsill. "We deserve to hear the story tonight, Bobby. We have spent many, many lonely days waiting for you to return."

Bobby was tired. The things that had happened in the past few days had left him totally exhausted. He remembered hearing one of Remington's friends during the Christmas party last year say he was "bummed out." Remington had explained it meant really tired and not wanting to do anything. That was exactly how he felt.

Then he suddenly felt ashamed of himself. He had the opportunity to travel and see lots of different things while his family remained alone in the apartment for more than two weeks.

"You are right, Uncle Flicker. In fact, all of you are. You deserve to hear what happened. When Remington is asleep, I will tell you, but you will have to listen very closely. It is an amazing story, and Mr. McGillicuddy is

fortunate he didn't get hurt. And, as for what happened to me, I thought maybe I wouldn't tell you, but I guess I better. I'm lucky to even be here to tell the story. Shhh! Remington's coming out of the bathroom. He will be in bed in a few seconds, and I bet it doesn't take him long to get to sleep."

Within a couple of minutes Bobby's prediction came true. Even though he was only ten years old, Remington could sure snore. His mom had kidded him for the last four or five years, telling him many times that he must have learned how to snore from his daddy.

Well, whoever he had learned it from, he had learned it well and was snoring very, very loudly. Across the room on the windowsill, Bobby finally said to his family, *"He's certainly asleep now. So, here goes. This is what happened to Mr. McGillicuddy, and then I will tell you what happened to me."*

"To you? Oh, no!"

"Take it easy, Mom. I'm okay now, and I promise to tell the whole story."

Remington tossed and turned, but after a few minutes he settled down and snored only occasionally. Soon, a smile crept across his face. He was deep in sleep, but it

was like the whole trip he had taken was passing in front of him. He smiled even more as his dream became reality.

"Grandpa, come with me. I want to show you the castle."

"We can't just leave, Remington. Let's just wait outside this shop. They will be finished in a few minutes."

"Grandpa. Can't you see through this door? They are still in there looking at every purse, notebook, and suitcase in the store. See! Even dad is looking at stuff. Are you interested in those things? You weren't looking at them when we were in there."

"Well, not really," Mr. McGillicuddy said with a sigh. "No, not really."

"Then let's go. We told them we might start walking up toward the castle. Plus, Dad said the castle closes at five thirty, and it's already almost four o'clock."

"Is it that late?"

"Yes. It says so right here on my new watch you gave me for my birthday."

"Ok, you win. We won't wait for grandma and your folks. They will find us. Do you have that booklet with all the information on things to see?"

"Yes. Come on. Don't worry. It's just right up there." Remington pointed past a long row of shops and tiny stores with lots of souvenirs sitting on tables and display shelves on the sidewalks in front of them. "I know my way around the castle. Mom and Dad and I came here and visited last September."

Mr. McGillicuddy was paying little attention. He was trying to catch his breath as he climbed up the hill. "It's tough walking on these old cobblestones. They are hard on my feet, and I keep slipping. So slow down, Remington."

"Oh, Grandpa, don't be so silly. I'm not walking fast. You are walking slower. Anyway, see, we are almost there. That's the entrance where the guard is standing by that huge doorway. And there's the ticket booth right next to it. Let's just buy our own tickets. Mom, Dad, and Grandma can get theirs when they get here."

Moments later Remington and his granddad were in the castle's main hallway. "I already remember some things from my last trip here. Let's skip this first room and go to the next one because it has all kinds of neat things."

Remington tugged his grandfather into a room that looked like something out of a nightmare.

Mr. McGillicuddy's eyes were wide open immediately. "Oh, Remington, look at that wooden table. See those openings for two hands and a head? They actually put prisoners in those things and then screwed the holes so tight that they couldn't move their hands or head."

Remington looked for a moment and then dashed around a corner and hollered, "Look at those big iron balls and the spikes on the outside. Did they fight people with those things, Grandpa?"

"Oh, yes. But they also used them to torture and beat prisoners."

"Was that after they stabbed them with these swords?" Remington asked and pointed up to a knight sitting on top of a horse with a very, very long weapon in his hand that stretched to the ground.

"Oh, I'm sure there were plenty of soldiers wounded and killed by those things," Mr. McGillicuddy answered. "Actually it is a lance and not a sword."

In the next ten minutes the pair walked in and out of small little caves or rooms set back from the main room, and in each were different, terrible pieces of machinery or weapons used to fight and torture.

"Grandpa, this room reminds me of some of the stuff we saw at Christmastime when we were in the museum at the Royal Palace."

"You're right. It sure does. Why don't we just sit down here and rest for a moment? It's been a long day, and we can keep an eye out for your parents. I know you were here last year, but do you remember why this castle was built on this high cliff above the Mediterranean Sea?" Before Remington could answer, Mr. McGillicuddy added, "I had a chance to read a booklet about it that was in our bedroom."

Mr. McGillicuddy had his grandson's attention. He sat back, and adjusted his left shoulder so it nudged in between two large stones in the wall. Now that he was comfortable, he smiled and continued, taking his time remembering things he had read.

"...And finally, the castle itself was built over eight hundred years ago. So lots of different people from many other countries have lived here during all these centuries." He looked at his grandson. "So pretty interesting, huh?"

"Yes, except you forgot to tell me the answer to the first question. Why was it built on this high, high, giant rock that overlooks the sea?"

"Well, get up from this hard old bench we're on and run over to that window over there and tell me what you see."

Remington hopped up and dashed to the opening in the stone wall. He peered down and then turned around with a puzzled look on his face. He plodded back to the bench, clearly deep in thought. "I don't know. I mean it's what we've already seen. We are way up high, really high above the water, and there are a bunch of rocks beneath the castle."

"Good, Remi. So the castle is very high above the sea with many jagged rocks beneath. Can you guess why that is?"

Remington shook his head.

"Well, it would be difficult to climb up here, wouldn't it? The people who first built the castle picked this spot because it was the easiest to defend. It would be nearly impossible for someone to get to the top without being killed before reaching the castle. There have been a lot of wars and battles since the castle was built, and lots of different leaders have ruled from here, but the most interesting one was a pope."

"What's a *pope*, Grandpa?"

"I know you're not Catholic, but surely you have heard of the pope."

Remington shook his head. "No. Are you almost done, Grandpa? I want to walk around some more. And I don't know why mom, dad, and grandma aren't here yet."

"Oh, I'm sure they will be soon. Yes, we can walk some more, but don't you want to hear about the pope?

"Oh, okay, I guess."

"He lives in Rome, Italy, and he is the leader of millions and millions of Catholics throughout the world. Today there is only one pope, but hundreds of years ago there were some Catholics who wanted a different pope. That pope needed a safe place to live because most Catholics didn't like him. So he and his followers left Italy and came here to *Peñiscola*. They were here for many years, but finally there were large armies that came to capture him and they attacked the castle."

"You mean right here?"

151

"Yes."

"I thought you said the rocks to the sea made it impossible to get up here."

"Oh, there were other ways. The armies fought their way up the same hill that we walked up today. Here in the castle the Pope's followers and his army threw boiling oil and other liquids out through the openings in the walls. It sprayed down on the attackers and burned them badly. They shot arrows and they had huge wooden slingshots that threw huge rocks down on the men charging up the road. Hundreds were killed. But the army still made it here to the top, and they captured the pope. They took him away, and then there was only one pope for the world."

Remington sat with his eyes and mouth wide open. Mr. McGillicuddy reached underneath Remington's jaw with the thumb and forefinger of both of his hands and playfully closed his grandson's mouth. "You didn't know I knew so much, did you?"

Remington shook his head. Then his grandpa smiled. "Well, I read part of it and the other part I made up, but the pope really was run out of here."

Suddenly Remington jumped off the bench they were seated on. "Look! I told you they would get here. Here comes our family."

"Well, it was really me who said they would get here," laughed Mr. McGillicuddy.

Remington waved and shouted. "Grandma, Dad, Mom. Here we are over here." They were at the other end of the long, wide, stonewalled hallway that stretched in front of seven rooms. His mom waved back and started walking toward him.

"Come on, Grandpa." Remington ran down the hall toward his mother.

When Remington got to his mom, he gave her a big hug, and he reached in and pulled Bobby out of his pocket. "See," he told her, "Bobby and I and Grandpa have been touring the castle together."

"We were worried about you when we first got here," she said. "We couldn't find you. We've been walking in and out of every room looking for you."

"It isn't that big of a castle."

"Still big enough to get lost in, and you didn't really tell us you were coming here."

"Yes, we did. Remember? Grandpa said we were going to go outside and wait for you on the steps in front of that store, and I said we might go on to the castle and meet you. You even smiled and said 'okay.'"

"I think you made some of that up. I'm not sure I said that."

"Well, we probably wouldn't have remembered," said Mrs. McGillicuddy. "We were having too much fun looking at all those pretty leather bags. That nice lady named

Terri was too good of a sales lady. She owned the store and she sold us a lot of things."

"I should have gone with you," said Remington's dad.

"Wow, Dad! How many sacks have you got hanging on your shoulder?"

"More than I should," he said with a laugh. "In each bag there is a new purse for your grandma and mom and I even have a gift for you and granddaddy."

"Really. From that store you found a gift for me?"

"Oh, yeah. You will be surprised, and so will your grandfather. Where is he? I don't see him. Is he okay?"

"He's back there, sitting down in one of the rooms at the end of the hall. He was getting tired."

"Well, let's go get him because it is five twenty-five, and one of the guards in the room we just left told everyone that it was time to leave the castle."

"I'll go get Granddad."

"Oh, that's okay. Let's hurry up and we'll all go down there. We can leave by that side door exit at the end of the hall, anyway."

Remington walked down the hall with his parents, and when they reached the end, they looked in the last room, but Mr. McGillicuddy wasn't there. Just at that moment, an announcement came over the loudspeaker advising everyone they needed to leave the building now.

Mrs. McGillicuddy became nervous. "Oh, my, they can't close the door and lock it with him still in here."

154

Remington's dad said, "I will go back where we just were and check each of those rooms. Plus, I can talk to the guards in Spanish if they cause me any trouble. The rest of you go out this exit right here. He's going to be fine. I will find him."

The others left, but Remington suddenly remembered the room that Mr. McGillicuddy had liked the most. Even though his mom told him not to, he turned and ran past a guard and back into the castle. The guard started running after him, but he was too fat, and Remington had an easy time getting away.

Remington ran into the big room with the torture equipment, where he thought he would find Mr. McGillicuddy, but he wasn't there.

Remington suddenly sat up in the bed. His eyes were closed, and his head tilted downward. Suddenly a giant sneeze whipped his head upward. Blankly he peered around the room, his owlish eyes wide open, before lying back down.

Within two minutes he was lightly snoring again.

Now deep in sleep, Remington suddenly rolled to his right and a frown flit across his face.

Remington saw two tall guards, who were much younger, come running into the room he had raced into. He heard

lots of words in Spanish, but they were talking too fast for him to understand. Although he was certain everything being said had to do with him.

He was hiding behind an old cannon near an opening that looked down into the sea. He knew within minutes, if not seconds, he would probably be found. Then a thought came to him, and he reached in his pocket and pulled the blue bulb out. "Bobby, go find him and fly back and show me where he is."

Then he placed the blue bulb on a big, huge, iron ball with spikes in it, and he ran toward the guards. He turned around and looked back for a moment and motioned for Bobby to get out of there.

Bobby paused and watched Remington tossing and turning. He was just about to continue telling his story when Flicker's voice boomed from the other end of the strand. "*When do we get to the part where you are the hero, Bobby?*"

"*Will you be quiet?*" Aunt Shining stared over her bifocals at her husband.

"*Once the guards had left the room, I yelled 'puhrumba' and started to lift off the iron ball. It was then I realized I was in real trouble.*"

"Oh, my heavens!" Shining raised her voice again from the opposite end. "What happened then, Bobby?"

"Well, I suddenly saw I was trapped in the torture room because the guards had closed the door, and there was no way I could open it. But I flew over to the door anyway, just to be sure, and then I knew for certain. It was then I looked up toward the ceiling, which was really high, and I saw a tiny little window in the corner. I had to see if I could escape that way, so I yelled 'puhrumba' two more times, and I took off flying toward that opening. As I got closer, I saw it really wasn't a window but an open space with iron bars like they have in a jail.

"It was lucky for me because I now knew there was at least a way out of the room, and I would be able to fly outside and find Remington. I decided to drift back down near the floor and rest for a moment. I was going to need all the energy I could get.

"But just as I landed in a chair, I heard a noise."

"What was it?" shouted Energizer.

"It is the same as the one each of you has been hearing, from Remington for the last hour."

"You mean, snoring?"

"Yes, Aunt Glaring. That was the sound. Someone was snoring.

"When I heard it, I thought of Mr. McGillicuddy drinking eggnog at Christmas, falling asleep and snoring in front of the television set."

"So. Where was Mr. McGillicuddy?"

Aunt Glaring frowned at Flicker and whispered, "Stop your bellowing and listen."

Bobby smiled. "Not very far away, but you don't know the funny part of the story yet."

"Well, then tell it right now."

Bobby chuckled for a moment, picturing the scene in his mind. "When I said 'puhrumba!' and lifted off the bench, I only flew a few feet before I saw him hidden in a corner."

Once more he started laughing, and took another moment to compose himself before he continued.

"There he was leaning on a strange-looking piece of equipment that had been used to torture prisoners by placing their hands and necks through openings that were then closed by tightening screws. The pressure caused terrible pain for the criminal.

"Of course, Mr. McGillicuddy wasn't a prisoner, and he had simply placed both hands through the openings and laid his head down on top of the wooden block. Since there wasn't anybody tightening screws or torturing him, he was enjoying a very sound sleep. I could tell because his snoring got louder and louder the closer I got to him.

"My problem was I couldn't wake him up, and the guards weren't coming back in that room. So I had to get out of the room and find Remington and his mom and dad. If they didn't find him, then he was going to be one scared

old man when he woke up in the middle of the night, alone in the pitch-black darkness of the castle. So I yelled 'puhrumba' three times, as loud as I could, and then I flew toward the ceiling and those two iron bars."

"*How did you get through the window, dear?*"

Bobby looked at his mom and smiled. "*Well it was easy because there was no glass and just the two bars with lots of space between the sides. I just slipped through and then I started flying down toward the ground. I stayed close to the castle wall, and I guess Remington had been looking for me, because I spotted him waving just a few seconds after I had escaped the room.*"

Bobby saw his sister, Twinkle, stretching out from the strand and tilting forward in her pod. "*How were you able to tell Remington where his grandfather was?*"

Bobby started to explain and then said, "*Shh!*" Most of the bulbs looked across the room and there was a soft chuckle rippling through the strand. Remington had sat up in the bed like he had done earlier. His head had fallen backward and then quickly forward, but this time there was no sneezing.

The soft snoring started again, he twitched slightly, and a smile broke out on his face.

Remington saw his dad step through the side entrance where his mom and grandma were waiting.

"Where is he?" asked Mrs. McGillicuddy.

"Couldn't find him, Mom. I looked everywhere."

Mrs. McGillicuddy had a troubled expression on her face as she peered over a stone wall and looked down at the miles of beaches and seaside hotels. "You don't think there is a chance he wandered away while we were in there and is walking around in this part of the town?"

I don't think so, Grandma. He said he was so sleepy and tired, that he could lie down and fall asleep anyplace. So, why would he go for a walk?"

His dad nodded his head in agreement. "What you say makes sense, but we still can't find him. Even the guards helped me. We searched every room except the one with the torture equipment. That's the one they chased you into, and you are sure you didn't see him in there?"

"I am sure."

"I hope you are right because it's the one place I didn't look."

The two guards walked back up to the group, and Remington's dad began speaking rapidly in Spanish. Remington could only understand a little, but he knew he was asking them if they would take him back one more time to check the torture room. They were shaking their heads sideway. The answer was no.

It was then Remington heard the words for U.S. Embassy, and he was sure his dad was trying to impress them so they would open the doors, but they continued to shake their heads.

Mrs. McGillicuddy stood to the side crying, and Remington's mom wrapped her arms around her.

With everyone occupied with arguing or crying, Remington knew this was the moment he needed. He knew for certain only Bobby could help save or find his granddad. He quickly walked past the museum door that was at the edge of the castle, and he ducked around the corner and out of sight. He wasn't sure why he had come this way, but he sort of remembered seeing a window at the top of this side of the castle. When he looked up, he saw he was right. There it was, and there were two small iron bars spaced a few inches apart. He was sure it must be the same window that was at the top of the torture room. If Bobby found Mr. McGillicuddy, then this would be the way he would fly to find Remington.

He peeked back around the side of the building. His dad and the guards were now talking to another man who had joined the group. He was wearing a suit and a tie, and he looked important. His mom was still hugging his grandmother. *Good*, he thought, *if they stay busy, maybe they won't notice I'm gone.* He turned back around and stared up at the window. *I just wish Bobby would fly out of that window and find me.* He peeked around the corner one more time to make sure no one was looking for him, and when he turned back around, he had gotten his wish.

When he looked up, he saw the blue bulb descending from below the window. It was Bobby, and if he had just

flown out of that window, then it surely meant he knew something about his grandfather. He looked around to see if any of the tourists walking nearby were looking up at the side of the castle. He didn't notice anybody watching, and he was glad because less than five seconds later, Bobby fell right into his hand.

Remington wasted no time. They had to hurry because he didn't think his dad had convinced those guards and policemen to let them inside for one more try.

"Is he there, Bobby? Did you find him?"

Bobby quickly tilted himself into a sitting position and tilted forward and backward.

"You did. Oh, boy! That's great. What room did you find him in?"

As soon as he asked the question, he knew it was stupid. How could Bobby tell him? But Bobby did in his own way.

The bulb quickly shook from side to side. And then he did it again.

"I know," squealed Remington. "You didn't find him in another room, right?"

Bobby tipped himself forward and backward.

"I got it. You found him in the torture room, right?"

Bobby once more tipped himself forward and backward.

"Quick, we've got to let Dad know," and Remington squeezed Bobby tightly in his hand and ran around the corner. Just a few yards away, he could see the man in

the suit. He was shaking hands with his dad and was now walking away.

He started running and yelling. "Dad, I've found him. I found him." Then he realized what he had said, and he started to explain that Bobby had found him, but he had already reached his father. "Daddy, Grandpa is in the torture room someplace."

"How do you know that?"

"Yes, Remington, how do you know that?" his grandmother said as she rushed to his side.

"Bobby just told me."

"Oh, Remington, not now. The bulb didn't tell you."

"You better believe it, Mom. He just flew out of the castle and told me." Remington paused for a moment and then stammered and said, "Well, he didn't exactly say it, but he did let me know where Grandpa is."

"And how did he do that?" she asked.

"I can't explain it, just believe me. I'll explain later."

"Well, we don't have anything to lose, but I am going to have to tell a lie," his dad said, and he hurried down the cobblestone, yelling at the man in the suit to stop.

Within a minute he had returned and he rushed up to the three of them.

"He's going to do it."

"You mean he's going to open the castle doors?"

"That's exactly what I mean. I told him my son had confessed that his grandfather had told him he was going to take a nap in the torture room."

"I never said that, Daddy."

"I know you didn't, but be quiet for now. It's the only way he would agree to tell the guards to unlock the doors. And see"—Remington's dad pointed to the small door just a few feet away—"they are opening the side entrance right now."

Less than five minutes later the guards walked back outside through that same door and trailing behind them with a grin on his blushing face came Mr. McGillicuddy. Remington was the first to reach him, and he jumped into his arms.

Remington sat straight up in the bed. He opened his eyes. His arms were stuck out in front of him like he was trying to hold on to somebody. He was confused only for a couple of seconds, and then he started laughing.

"Wow! Wait until I tell grandpa about this dream. It was just like I was in that castle again."

He looked at the clock. It read 9:25.

"Boy, I was tired."

He jumped out of bed and put on his house shoes and raced out the door. "I've got to tell grandpa about the dream."

Bobby watched Remington leave the room. He was curious about what he had heard him say about the castle. He wondered if Remington had been dreaming about the same story he had spent the night telling his family.

Well, whether he had or hadn't it didn't matter. He knew he still had an even bigger story to tell.

"So, you want to hear what happened to me?"

The shouts came from throughout the strand.

"Yes."

"Tell us the whole story."

"Tell us what happened to you."

"That's exactly what I'm going to do. Although I think Dad and Aunt Glaring had better keep an eye on my mom. She is going to panic before this story is over."

And then he recalled the amazing tale of how he almost never returned to his family again.

19
Time to Go Home

"The three weeks have gone too quickly," Mrs. McGillicuddy said. "I wish we had agreed with you when you told us to plan to stay for a whole month."

"I know, dear, it's my fault," said Mr. McGillicuddy. "We will never get to see Spain again."

"Oh, don't ever say *never*, Grandpa. Plus, remember this: we will all be back together again in the United States when we come home in November."

"I know. Tell you what, my favorite grandson—"

"Grandpa, I am your only grandson."

Everyone standing around the dining room table laughed.

"Well, you are still my favorite. Anyway, I was just going to say that we should try to make the time go faster."

"How do you do that?"

"Well...uhh...I guess I was just kidding about that too, Remington."

"If we all keep busy," Remington's mom said, "before we know it, we will be back at Grandma and Grandpa's for Christmas. You can play with Rocket, and you'll have your own little tree in the upstairs bedroom again." She paused and looked at Mr. and Mrs. McGillicuddy. "I guess I should ask if you are planning to have a tree for him again."

"Well, of course we will, Lisa. Remington, you will have your own tree in that room until you think you are too old to have one."

"Thanks, Grandma, and both of you be careful with Bobby and the bulbs. Make sure you take care of them."

"We will do it, I promise."

Mr. McGillicuddy reached down and picked up his grandson. "You know, I was just curious. With that magical blue bulb helping to find me and you loving him so much, I was wondering if you'd like for me to leave him here and I will take the rest of the bulbs home. They will be on the tree when you get there for Christmas, and you can put Bobby on the strand."

Remington moved backwards in the arms of his grandfather and leaned back to look him in the face. "That's a good idea, but it's okay. We've been together a lot and he would want to be with his family. He would miss the other bulbs."

"You're sure?"

Remington paused for a couple of seconds and then nodded. "I'm sure."

"Everybody ready to go to the airport," Remington's dad said as he walked into the room. "I have everything packed in the car, and we need to get downstairs. You know how narrow the street is, and I have the car parked on the sidewalk."

Maria came running into the room. "I will mees all of you so much."

"I'm not going anyplace, Maria, just to the airport."

"Oh, Remington. You know, I mean your *abuelos*, I mean your grandparents." She reached up and hugged both Mr. and Mrs. McGillicuddy. "I am sorry I was not weeth you on the vacation, but I needed to be weeth my friends in the North where I from."

Mrs. McGillicuddy patted her arm. "We understand. Plus, we are looking forward to having you come to America."

A huge smile broke across Maria's face. "I looking forward too, *señora*. I am happy to learn they want me with them."

"Maria, we will always want you with us, but we've got to get going to the airport right now," said Remington's dad, and he hurried out the door as his parents followed behind him.

When they reached the elevator, Mr. and Mrs. McGillicuddy turned and waved to Maria. They saw her wipe a

170

handkerchief across her eyes before she returned the wave. She shouted, "You will have surprises for me in America?"

"Yes, we will," Mrs.McGillicuddy shouted back as she stepped into the elevator.

But neither lady could imagine how many surprises there would be.

Epilogue

Mr. McGillicuddy gently placed the bulbs inside one of the pockets of a small carry-on suitcase and then pulled the flap over and zipped it up. When he had finished, he closed the suitcase and picked it up. He carried it out of the bedroom and down the steps to the first floor. Inside, Bobby lay very still. Mr. McGillicuddy had wrapped the bulbs tightly together with a rubber band to make sure they were secure and would not bounce around.

Bobby knew when Mr. McGillicuddy had reached the living room. There was a slight bump as he sat the suitcase down. He could hear voices and a couple of times, he definitely recognized Remington's. At that moment, Bobby wished he could see Remington again, but that wouldn't happen until a few days before Christmas.

As for his family, there was nothing that could be said to make any of the bulbs feel better. He heard the sobbing of his mom, and with the bulbs wrapped in a tight circle, he was able to easily hear his Aunt Shining, who was normally much further away. She, too, was crying softly. And he knew that both of his sisters had also cried earlier in the morning. There was no question about

it. Life was going to change for the whole Bobby Bright family. Those old days of being locked away in a closet were about to happen again. All of his family would miss the freedom they had enjoyed in Spain and the wonderful chance to actually shine and glow at least part of almost every day.

When he stopped and thought about it, he knew that he had been very, very fortunate to be with Remington. They had traveled to many places and done many things. He would miss being around his good buddy almost every day. And, there was no question that he was going to miss those funny-sounding times when each of them, to the best of their abilities, had tried to say a few words in the other's language.

These months had been very special, but suddenly, Bobby felt guilty. He had experienced so many more exciting moments than the other bulbs, and yet, they were always thanking him for the freedom they had enjoyed. He hoped he hadn't been selfish.

Now, as the suitcase was lifted off the floor, he realized the truth. He knew that after all of the excitement in the past seven months, he felt worn out and tired. He was looking forward to resting and doing nothing.

Outside in the hallway, the suitcase gently bumped against Mr. McGillicuddy's leg as he walked into the elevator. Bobby heard Mrs. McGillicuddy's voice. She was yelling goodbye to Maria.

Deep in the suitcase, Bobby Bright softly whispered, "I think I may be happy to be back in a closet and away from humans for a while."

But little did he know that what was about to happen in less than six months from now would make him forever wish he had never spoken those words.

flip me over

flip me over

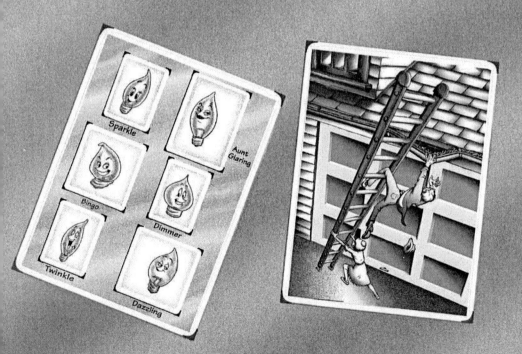